Emily Harvale lives in Ea
although she would prefer
Alps…or Canada…or anywhere that has several
months of snow. Emily loves snow almost as much
as she loves Christmas.

Having worked in the City (London) for several
years, Emily returned to her home town of
Hastings where she spends her days writing. And
wondering if it will snow.

You can contact her via her website, Twitter,
Facebook or Instagram.

There is also a Facebook group where fans can
chat with Emily about her books, her writing day
and life in general. Details are on the 'For You'
page of Emily's website.

Author contacts:
www.emilyharvale.com
www.twitter.com/emilyharvale
www.facebook.com/emilyharvalewriter
www.instagram.com/emilyharvale

\*\*\*

Scan the code above to see all Emily's books on Amazon

# Also by this author

Highland Fling
Lizzie Marshall's Wedding
The Golf Widows' Club
Sailing Solo
Carole Singer's Christmas
Christmas Wishes
A Slippery Slope
The Perfect Christmas Plan
Be Mine
It Takes Two
Bells and Bows on Mistletoe Row

**The Goldebury Bay series**:
Ninety Days of Summer – book 1
Ninety Steps to Summerhill – book 2
Ninety Days to Christmas – book 3

**The Hideaway Down series**:
A Christmas Hideaway – book 1
Catch A Falling Star – book 2
Walking on Sunshine – book 3
Dancing in the Rain – book 4

**Hall's Cross series**
Deck the Halls – book 1
The Starlight Ball – book 2

**Michaelmas Bay series**
Christmas Secrets in Snowflake Cove – book 1
Blame it on the Moonlight – book 2

**Lily Pond Lane series**
The Cottage on Lily Pond Lane –
Part One – New beginnings and Summer secrets
Part Two – Autumn leaves and Trick or treat
Christmas on Lily Pond Lane
Return to Lily Pond Lane
A Wedding on Lily Pond Lane

# Secret Wishes

and

Summer Kisses

on

Lily Pond Lane

Emily Harvale

Copyright © 2019 by Emily Harvale.

Emily Harvale has asserted her right to be identified as the author of this work.

No part of this publication may be reproduced, stored in a retrieval system, or transmitted, in any form or by any means, electronic, mechanical, photocopying, recording or otherwise, without the prior written permission of the publisher.

This book is a work of fiction. Names, characters, organisations, businesses, places and events other than those clearly in the public domain, are either the product of the author's imagination or are used fictitiously. Any resemblance to actual persons, living or dead, events or locales is entirely coincidental.

ISBN 978-1-909917-44-6

Published by Crescent Gate Publishing

Print edition published worldwide 2019
E-edition published worldwide 2019

Editor Christina Harkness

Cover design by JR and Emily Harvale

In memory of Ann Kellett.
An inspiration to everyone who knew her.

Acknowledgements

My grateful thanks go to the following:

Christina Harkness for her patience and care in editing this book.
My webmaster, David Cleworth who does so much more than website stuff.
My cover design team, JR.
Luke Brabants. Luke is a talented artist and can be found at: www.lukebrabants.com
My wonderful friends for their friendship and love. You know I love you all.
All the fabulous members of my Readers' Club. You help and support me in so many ways and I am truly grateful for your ongoing friendship. I wouldn't be where I am today without you.
My Twitter and Facebook friends, and fans of my Facebook author page. It's great to chat with you. You help to keep me (relatively) sane!
Thank you for buying this book.

# Secret Wishes and Summer Kisses on Lily Pond Lane

# Chapter One

'You're in my pond.'

Tabbie Talbaine's hand shot to her chest as a grizzled old woman tapped on the driver's window with a long, twisted stick of wood.

'Gosh, you startled me!'

Tabbie let out a sigh of relief as she pressed the button to open the window and smiled as the stooped, thin figure glared at her.

Heavy set black brows flew up towards grey curls, loosely tied, but tumbling from what looked rather worryingly like a bone.

'I startled you? You scared the life out of me.' With the window now open, the woman used her stick to poke at Tabbie's seat.

'Please be careful with that stick.' Tabbie leant to one side. 'You could poke a person's eye out with that.'

'I'll do more than poke an eye out if you don't get this thing out of my pond and my garden right now.' She waved the stick menacingly.

Tabbie glanced around and took in her surroundings. Pond? What pond? Her beloved Smart Cabrio's front end was in a muddy hole, not a pond. The so-called garden was merely a field dotted with wild flowers and this large ditch was in the middle of what Tabbie had believed to be a lane, although the hedges surrounding it were so overgrown it was difficult to tell.

'I beg your pardon?'

'You'll do more than beg my pardon, missy. You'll be a-begging for your life if you're not gone within ten minutes.'

Tabbie sucked in a breath. 'I'm truly sorry but I can assure you this was an accident. I had no intention of driving into your … pond … or your garden. I thought this was a lane. And it may have escaped your attention but my car is head first in this dit– I mean, in your pond. It'll take more than ten minutes for the RAC to get here once I've been able to contact them.' She darted a glance at her phone. 'If I can ever get a signal, that is. I can't seem to get even one bar on my phone.'

'Useless thing. You may as well chuck that in my pond while you're at it, for all the good it'll do you in this neck of the woods.'

The woman's cackle wasn't comforting. Neither was the fact that twilight was chasing away the dying rays of the setting sun. It would be dark in a couple of hours. Was that enough time for Tabbie to get herself and her beloved car out of this ditch slash pond and as far away as possible from this rather scary woman? She wouldn't be out of place in a Stephen King novel although the woman's dark purple cloak lent itself more to witches and demons. Oh dear. Tabbie wished she hadn't let her mind wander in those directions. A quick glance around confirmed her fears. Not another human in sight apart from the old woman who was staring at her in a manner that indicated Tabbie was being measured in some way. Perhaps for a coffin ... or a cooking pot?

'Don't be ridiculous, woman,' Tabbie mumbled.

'Ridiculous?' The woman's screech set Tabbie's teeth on edge. 'You cheeky miss. You've got the nerve to call me names when you're the one who's driven her car into *my* pond?'

'I'm sorry. I wasn't calling you names. I was talking to myself.' The woman might be old but her hearing was exceptional.

'Hmm. So you're mad as well as being a bad driver. But I'm not afraid of the likes of you, missy.'

Tabbie hadn't meant to laugh. It was probably nerves. But come on. Didn't the woman have a mirror? Only one person here looked like a character from a horror movie. And it wasn't Tabbie.

'You find that funny, do you?'

Tabbie shook her head. 'No, no. Believe me. I'm not finding any humour at all in this situation.'

'You laughed.'

'Nerves. Frustration. It's better than crying. I'm truly sorry. If you'll tell me where I can find a phone, I'll make a call and then I can get both myself and my car out of here as quickly as humanly possible. In fact, if you can tell me the way to Witt's Cottage, I'll be able to make a call from there, although I may need some assistance to get out of my car. The door–'

'Witt's Cottage? What do you want at Witt's Cottage?' The expression on the woman's face turned to one of shock.

'Not that it's any of your business but … sorry. That was impolite of me. I suppose I am trespassing as far as you're concerned.' Tabbie sighed and began again. 'I was on my way to Witt's Cottage to see my mother's friend and I thought this lane led there. That's what my Sat Nav assured me, so hopefully it can't be too far from here.'

The woman leant closer, her dark eyes narrowing and a dubious frown further creasing an already creased brow.

'Your mother's friend? Who are you? Who's your mother and what's the name of her friend?'

Tabbie gave a friendly smile. Perhaps that would work. The old woman's tone had mellowed slightly so Tabbie would try to build on that.

'My name's Tabitha. But my friends call me Tabbie. My mother is Camilla Talbaine Saint Sorrel and her friend is Aurelia Jenkins who lives in Witt's Cottage.'

The woman's mouth formed a perfect 'O' but her shaking head implied she found it difficult to believe. She stared at Tabbie for a moment longer before suddenly slapping her thigh and bursting into laughter. Well, more of a cackle. She swayed back and forth and waved her stick wildly in the air. It was several seconds before she spoke but when she did her manner was transformed. As if someone had cast a spell, turning the woman from an ugly old witch into a friendly, charming and warm-hearted, fairy godmother.

'Well, knock me down with a bat's wing. You're Cami's daughter? I thought there was something familiar about you.'

'Cami?'

'Cami Talbaine. She never should've married that Simon Saint Sorrel. But would she listen? Not that I blame her. He looked like George Clooney and twice as smooth. Good thing he left after you were born. Still not heard from him? No, of course not. What's the point? Waste of good clean air keeping that man breathing.'

'Excuse me. That's my father you're talking about and although I know there were problems, my mother never says a bad word against him.'

'That's probably because she never says anything about him, does she?'

That was true. Camilla never spoke of Simon Saint Sorrel unless it was absolutely necessary. Even at an early age, Tabbie saw the flash of pain that would shoot into her mother's eyes at the mention of his name.

Tabbie shook her head. 'No. But how did you know that? Do you know my mother? Or has her friend Mrs Jenkins spoken of her?'

'Know your mother? Of course I know Cami. We were like two peas in a pod.' The smile faded. 'Until Simon Saint Sorrel. But it's too late in the day to talk about that.' She shook her head and sucked in a quick breath. 'Why are you sitting in that car? Get out and come and have some tea. You can call the RAC from my cottage.'

Realisation dawned but Tabbie couldn't quite believe it. '*You're* Aurelia Jenkins? *You're* my mother's friend?' The woman looked nothing like the one in the photographs that Camilla had shown her. But they were old photos taken at least forty years ago. Even so, if this woman was Aurelia Jenkins, she had changed beyond recognition.

Aurelia nodded. 'Hard to believe? Time has painted a somewhat sorry canvas. Don't even recognise myself at times when I look in the mirror. But do come along, Tabbie. Don't sit there all day. That pond is deeper than it looks and that tiny car of yours might go under any minute.'

'What?' Tabbie was horrified but she tried to remain calm. 'The door's stuck in the mud and I can't get out. I've tried. Several times.'

She tried again, shoving her shoulder against it and using her full weight. Which wasn't much. She was slim. Too slim, she'd been told. Apart from her large bust. But why was she thinking about such things now? She might drown at any minute and this old woman, or Mrs Jenkins if that was really who she was, was unlikely to be able to get the door open. Tabbie glanced up at the closed, retractable roof. Would she have to open it and clamber out that way?

Aurelia smiled but she didn't step forward or make any attempt to assist Tabbie.

'Try once more.'

Tabbie frowned, took a deep breath and this time when she leant against the door, not only did it shoot open, but she tumbled out, landing on her knees in the mud.

'I don't believe it!'

She beamed up at the woman who leant both hands, together with her chin, on the top of her stick.

'Sometimes all you need is to want something enough to make it happen.' She turned away, still smiling. 'Grab your things, in case the car goes under, and follow me. It's been a long time since I've had company so you'll have to excuse the mess. I hope you're not allergic to cats because I have one or two who live with me. And one or two who come and go as they please.' She glanced over her shoulder. 'Oh, are you praying? Righty-oh. Follow me when you're ready. It's this way.' She pointed ahead with her stick and strode forward.

'I'm not praying,' Tabbie said, to Aurelia's back. 'I think I'm simply in a state of shock.'

A bubbling sound followed by a loud squelch soon made her move. She only had time to grab her handbag and her phone before clambering to safety on dry ground. Getting to her feet she turned and watched her beloved orange car sink into the water like a chunk of pumpkin in a pot of soup, until only the black retractable roof could be seen above the muddy water.

Now she wasn't sure who to call. The RAC, or a diver.

'Don't worry about that,' Aurelia called out, without so much as turning her head. 'I know a man or two who can get it out, and with a wash and a brush it'll be as good as new.'

Aurelia was clearly mad. It would take a lot more than a wash and a brush to make the car even usable again, let alone as good as new. It would take a miracle. Or magic. Neither of which Tabbie believed in.

But she did believe in insurance. Perhaps that was the call she should make? The insurance company would advise her what action she should take.

Experiencing a tiny glimmer of hope, she squished and squelched her way behind Aurelia.

What would Witt's Cottage be like? As untidy and unkempt as the owner? Aurelia had warned her about the mess. Thankfully, Tabbie wasn't allergic to cats. A number of images popped into her head, all of them rather unpleasant and one or two had not just cats, but frogs and toads and bats and …

Tabbie shivered. Not merely from the cold although the weather was unseasonably chilly for June but she was soaking wet from her tumble in Aurelia's so-called pond. Would there be central heating in this messy cottage? Or at the very least a fire?

She gasped as she followed Aurelia out from a small copse of trees into the twilight and saw Witt's Cottage. Why hadn't she spotted it from her car? It was only a few metres away. But it was not at all what she was expecting. It was like something out of a fairy tale.

The façade was the palest salmon pink beneath a thatched roof, which may have seen better days but somehow simply added to the overall charm of the place. The front garden burst with flowers and the four windows – two either side of the sky-blue front door, each had window boxes filled to the brim with more rainbow-coloured blooms. What really caught Tabbie's eye and gave her a warm and cosy feeling, was the pale shaft of grey smoke wafting from the salmon pink chimney. That meant there was at least a fire in Witt's Cottage.

Aurelia opened the door on to a bright pink hall. Not the pale salmon of the exterior but a vivid cerise pink. The wooden floor with its mellow, almost ivory wash was barely visible beneath a multicoloured hall runner. Frames jostled for space on the uneven walls but Tabbie noticed as she followed Aurelia towards what was probably the kitchen, judging by the heavenly aromas filling the air, that not all of them contained pictures. Several of the frames contained what appeared to be poems; some contained phrases and one or two seemed to contain recipes of some sort – but not for anything Tabbie could ever imagine eating.

She peered into what was perhaps the sitting room as they passed, and saw shelves crammed with old, leather bound books, two exceedingly comfy looking winged chairs piled high with colourful cushions and a couple of seemingly contented cats curled on the seats. Beyond them stood a large, blackened hearth where a welcoming fire crackled and spat as if it laughed at her appearance.

'This way,' Aurelia said, leading Tabbie into a room that resembled a scullery from Tudor times more than it did a kitchen. There was another roaring fire but this one had a large pot hanging above it from an iron hook and frame. There were no kitchen cupboards but there was an antique oak dresser and rows of matching shelves cut across uneven, white-washed walls. In the centre of the brick floor sat a large, equally ancient oak table and one solitary chair. As if reading Tabbie's mind, Aurelia added, 'I don't often have company.' But she grabbed a chair from out of nowhere and placed it on the fire side of the table. 'Sit there for a moment to dry off. I'll get you some clothes to change into until I can wash and dry your own. You're welcome to have a shower if you'd like one. Is that a twig in your hair?'

Tabbie's hand flew to her head and found the twig, teasing it out of her high, tight ponytail with care. Her hairdresser had copied the style from the fabulous Ariana Grande's signature design and had spent almost an hour that very morning perfecting the look to ensure that Tabbie's long, chestnut tresses were as sleek and perfect as the star's. A small, wet clump of mud came with the twig. Not so sleek now then.

Tabbie sighed. She dreaded to think what clothes Aurelia would give her to change into, but anything was better than mud-covered jeans and a sodden T-shirt – even if they were designer. And she'd love a shower but if this kitchen was anything to go by, the shower would probably be a bucket of cold water, and possibly, outside. Was the lavatory outside too? Oh, why did she have to think about that? Now she wanted to pee.

'I don't want to be a nuisance, Mrs Jenkins. Perhaps if I sit in front of the fire for a while, I'll soon be dry and if I can borrow your phone to call my insurers and the RAC, I'll be able to get my car out of your dit– pond and be on my way.'

Aurelia grinned. 'It does look more like a ditch than a pond at the moment, I'll admit. It's all the rain we've had recently together with the fact that I'm not as young as I was and I don't look after the garden as I should. But why the rush to leave? I thought you were on your way to pay me a visit. Why were you coming to see me? You didn't say. But you can tell me all that later. You're shivering. We must get you in a warm shower or you'll catch your death. Or perhaps a bath. Yes, a bath's the thing to have. I should've taken you directly to the bathroom. Follow me.'

Tabbie sighed again as Aurelia led the way back down the hall, this time turning halfway along and to Tabbie's surprise, opening a door from what appeared to be a solid wall. When Tabbie reached it she realised it was indeed a door, cleverly hidden. But why? Why hide a door?

The rickety flight of well-trodden stairs must have borne thousands of footfalls over the centuries. More images popped into Tabbie's head. This time of people, but all from long ago. How bizarre. It was because the cottage was so old. It was as if she had been transported back to a different era. Ridiculous, of course.

'How old is this cottage?'

'Oh my. It dates back to the 1600s. My great-great, well several greats actually, grandmother moved here from Lancashire in 1612.'

'From Lancashire? In 1612? Where in Lancashire?' Tabbie had recently written an article for her popular blog, *Tabbie Talbaine's Tasty Titbits*, regarding certain events in Lancashire in 1612, together with recipes from that time, and of course, local gossip from then and now.

Aurelia's back seemed to stiffen and she stopped on the top stair, turning to face Tabbie with a serious look in her eye.

'From Pendle Hill. And yes. Because of the Pendle Witch Trials. And yes. She was a witch, although she preferred to be known as a healer and an enabler, as all our family has.'

'A witch? You're teasing me, aren't you? And what's an–'

'No. I'm not. And I'll thank you not to laugh.' For a second, Aurelia's unpleasant demeanour returned but it was quickly gone. 'That was rude. I apologise. You were going to ask a question. Please ask it.'

'Um. I was merely going to ask what an enabler is? I know most so-called witches were simply healers and certainly used no magic spells, just herbs and plants to help people but I've never heard them referred to as enablers.'

A slight smile softened Aurelia's mouth and her whole body seemed to relax.

'My ancestors were all healers but we also help people in other ways. For example, if a person wants something, we might enable them to get it.'

'How, exactly?'

'Let's just say we help them find a way. We understand things many people do not and when a person has a problem, they can't see the wood for the trees. We ... help them see the light. Now, what would you like in your bath? Lavender's the most popular choice but I have my own concoction that I'm sure you'll love.'

Tabbie dismissed the image of bat's wing and

eye of newt and forced a smile.

'Lavender's fine, but I'm happy to try your potion. I mean, your product.'

Aurelia opened a door at the end of the hall and a large, white cast iron bath tub gleamed in the centre of a surprisingly spacious room. There was a fabulous, multi-jet, walk-in shower on one side and thankfully, a pristine-looking toilet – and, most astonishingly a bidet, on the other.

Tabbie blinked several times as she took it all in. The wall and floor tiles were almost the same salmon pink colour as the cottage exterior and it was only on closer inspection that she realised they were pink marble. Somewhat modern and luxurious not to mention expensive for an otherwise ancient cottage.

Aurelia handed her two sumptuous bath towels, a bar of what was clearly handmade soap with what appeared to be flower petals embedded in it, a flannel as soft as the towels and finally a beautiful etched balloon shaped, glass bottle containing the most divine fragrance Tabbie had ever smelt.

'What is this?'

Aurelia tapped the tip of her nose. 'A secret, family recipe. One the great, great grandmother I mentioned, Jennet de Witt, was famed for.'

'Jennet de Witt? Gosh. Is this cottage named after her? Or probably her husband?'

Aurelia nodded. 'It's named after her. She didn't have a husband. At least, not when she moved here. She bought the land, no mean feat in those days, and built the cottage herself.'

'She built it? Your ancestor built this cottage?'

Aurelia smiled. 'She did. Building the cottage was far simpler than buying the land, let me tell you. There have been a few changes and additions since then, of course, but a large part of it is almost exactly as it was in Jennet's day. I'll leave some clothes on the bed in the room next door. You can get dressed in there. In the meantime, I'll make a call to see if we can get your car out of my pond. Come down when you're ready and we can have a cup of my herbal tea. Then you can tell me what brought you here today.'

Clearly, like the topic of 'enablers' the conversation about Jennet was over.

'Oh yes. I was going to call the RAC, wasn't I? It went completely out of my head. That's very unlike me. I must still be in mild shock or something. Thank you for this, Mrs Jenkins.'

'It's Aurelia, and there's no need to thank me. Cami's daughter is more than welcome to anything in my hearth and home. Take as long as you want. I'll be downstairs. And I don't know about you but I'm getting a little peckish. I'll pop something in the pot.'

Tabbie didn't want to imagine what that might be.

# Chapter Two

Bree was having another mood swing and as usual, Garrick was being incredibly understanding and supportive. Almost annoyingly so.

'Why don't you sit down and relax, my darling?' He patted the back of one of the armchairs in front of the fire in the sitting room of Willow Cottage and beamed at her as torrential rain lashed the windowpanes and a gale force wind rattled the frames. 'I'll make dinner. And how about a nice cup of tea?'

'I can't relax.' Bree grabbed a stack of paperwork, held it upright and tapped the end repeatedly on the table to prove her point. 'It's been chucking it down virtually non-stop for days and the forecast for the weekend's really grim, with no let-up likely in the foreseeable future. I've got two weddings this weekend, both with marquees. One I've been able to rearrange to indoors but the other's in the middle of a field, so God alone knows where I'll find an alternative venue for that. I've been trying since this damn rain started. Next weekend I've got three, two of which are outdoors. It's June for heaven's sake. And my diary is chock-a-block. Everyone seems to be getting married this year. Over the next few months I've got twenty-five weddings to plan and execute. That's not counting ours.'

'But our wedding isn't until October so there's plenty of time to organise that.'

She glowered at him. 'Plenty of time? Are you mad?'

'You planned and organised Mia's wedding in less time and look what a great success that was. And it was your first and you didn't even have help. Well, none to speak of. Now you have three assistants. That's not counting me.'

His grin did nothing to placate her. 'I'll be the size of this cottage by October. Whose stupid idea was it to have our wedding then?'

'You weren't stupid to delay it until October, darling. I was the one who was being stupid for wanting to get married straightaway.'

Bree thumped the paperwork on the table and glowered harder. 'Don't patronise me, Garrick. We couldn't possibly get married before then. My business has surpassed all expectations, thanks to Mia and Jet, and I really need to focus.'

Undeterred, he walked towards her, his head tipped slightly to one side, his eyes filled with love, and a maddeningly sexy smile on his lips.

'I know, my darling. You want to concentrate

on your business and all of your clients' weddings without having to worry about your own. I understand that. But what you need right now, is to go to bed.'

'Don't look at me like that. That's how I got into this condition.' But she felt her lips curve into a smile. 'I'm sorry. I don't mean to be so moody and unreasonable. And I am, aren't I? Moody and unreasonable.'

'No more than anyone would be in your position. And I really don't mind. But I do mind you overdoing things. I know your business is important and I completely understand that it's your dream come true, but you need to watch your health, darling. The doctor said it's a miracle that you're pregnant, let alone with twins, but he also said we need to look after you. There must be more I can do to help with the business. And surely the team you got together for Mia and Jet's wedding know what they're doing now? Couldn't you let them and your assistants get on with it and simply supervise?'

Bree opened her mouth to argue but quickly closed it. Garrick was right. Yes, her wedding planning business, The Wright Wedding really was a dream come true. A dream that wouldn't have got off the ground if it hadn't been for Mia and Jet giving her the start-up funds, and with their ongoing investment, and all the bookings she had received as a result of their wedding, the business was already in profit.

But it had also been a dream of hers to have a child. An impossible dream, or so she had been told. Discovering she had fallen pregnant within a few weeks of dating Garrick was without doubt the biggest surprise of her life. And the most wonderful. Even more so than Mia and Jet's belief in her and her ability to make a success of The Wright Wedding.

Garrick wrapped his arms around her and she leant into his muscular chest, her heart beating wildly as it always did when she was in his arms. She looked up into his hazel eyes and ran her hand through his wonderfully thick, sandy brown hair.

'It's a miracle that you still love me after the way I've been behaving the last few weeks.'

He bent his head and kissed her softly on the lips.

'It's not your fault. It's your hormones. And I'll always love you no matter what. Besides, I've been through much worse. Ella's my twin sister, don't forget. When she gets mad you want to leave the country.' He grinned and kissed her again, for longer this time.

'Ella's lovely. You and I both know that.' She smiled up at him. 'I don't mean to be so horrid, I really don't. You're right though. It is my hormones. And morning sickness. I hadn't realised it would start so soon or be so dreadful. It's draining, in more ways than one. But there's so much I don't know about being pregnant, having never thought it would happen. Cathy and Christy gave me some tips. Apparently crackers, dry cereal and other bland carb-rich snacks all help. Which is why I'm eating so many of the damn things and putting on even more weight. You're supposed to keep something in your stomach at all times, according to them. And the ginger tea you suggested definitely helps.'

'Bear told me about that.'

She grinned at him. 'You're asking a vet for pregnancy advice?'

'Funny lady. He may only be a first responder but he knows quite a bit about it. And he is a first-class vet. Besides, let's not forget, he was the one who told you he thought you were pregnant when you thought you were having a heart attack.'

'I was teasing about asking him for advice. He's very knowledgeable.'

'I know. I told him to keep his diary for February pretty fluid, in case we can't get to the hospital and we need him to deliver our babies. Having delivered countless puppies, kittens, lambs, calves and the like, two little humans should be no trouble.'

Bree slapped him playfully on the arm before realising that might not be such a bad idea. If next February was as snowy as this February had been, getting to the hospital which was several miles away, might be a struggle.

But that was a frightening thought. What if there were complications? What if something went wrong? The pregnancy was a miracle; the births might not be. Even the nearest doctor was miles away. Bear was a fantastic vet, and a brilliant paramedic, but Bree didn't even want to contemplate having her babies anywhere other than in hospital, surrounded by experienced doctors and nurses, together with ample painkilling drugs, and the most up-to-date equipment possible.

She shared everything with Garrick except her fears. He had been through enough. Losing his previous girlfriend, Fiona in such a tragic way at the start of the year had devastated him. Bree knew better than most that he hadn't expected to fall in love again, and definitely not so soon. But in a way, she knew she had been his lifeline. He had his baby daughter, Flora, of course, who was the other love of his life, but Bree had given him hope for a future filled with love, laughter and happiness. A chance to have the family he so longed for. From the moment she had set eyes on Flora, she had loved the tiny bundle of joy as if the baby were her own. Imagine how Garrick would feel if Bree told him about her fears. Like her, he might begin to worry every time she felt an unexpected stab of pain. Or believed for one terrible moment that their babies had stopped moving. He was brimming over with happiness and love. She couldn't replace that with fear, or worry, or doubt. Subjecting him to her mood swings was bad enough.

'Perhaps we should also have Jet, Franklin and Pete on standby,' she joked, attempting to lighten her mood. 'All three of them have hands-on experience of delivering calves, so Mia told me.'

Garrick grinned. 'The more the merrier I say. Now please sit down while I go and make our dinner.'

'I'm not really hungry.'

'Neither am I as it happens. Shall I just make us a sandwich? You need to keep something in your stomach, remember?'

She pulled him closer and gave him her sexiest smile. 'Didn't you say something about me needing to go to bed?'

He tipped his head to one side. 'I did. But I thought you had paperwork.'

'I do. But it can wait.' She eased herself away from him and turned towards the stairs. 'Coming?'

He raised his brows and smiled broadly. 'I'll grab some crackers for later.'

'And pickles. I've got a craving for a giant gherkin.'

Garrick laughed and shook his head.

# Chapter Three

Hettie was definitely out of sorts. Even more so than she had been when she got her bad news the day before Mia and Jet's wedding. News she had kept to herself, other than sharing it with her husband Fred, of course.

But ever since the wedding something else had been niggling her – as if she didn't have enough to worry about already. And no matter how much she tried to ignore it, the feeling simply wouldn't go away.

The weather was not helping. It rained for three entire days after Mia and Jet departed for their honeymoon. That was followed by a few days of sunshine and showers. Then came the storms with gale force winds and temperatures more suited to November than June. Now it couldn't seem to make up its mind what it wanted to do. One minute the sky was blue and the sun appeared; the next there was torrential rain. One day there had been hail, a mini heatwave and something akin to a tornado, all within hours of each other.

But as she watched another sudden storm race in from the sea and rage outside her window before dissipating as it rolled inland, she knew it wasn't the weather that was niggling her, however weird it may be behaving. And rightly or wrongly she couldn't give a fig about Global Warming, so it certainly wasn't that.

Fred told her it was possibly because so much had changed in the village in such a short space of time and, on top of her other problem, it was upsetting her equilibrium, but what did he know? He had only lived in the village since moving in with her last September, and she had seen more changes in her lifetime than he could possibly imagine. As for change upsetting her equilibrium, that was stuff and nonsense.

Firstly, equilibrium was hardly a term that could be applied to her. Calm and balance had no place in her life. She would be the first to admit that dashing about to share the latest snippet of local gossip was far more important to her than peace and tranquillity.

Secondly, marrying Fred was a massive change, and she certainly wasn't upset about that. Far from it. After spending years in her cottage with only the ghost of her dead husband Hector for company, joined later by Prince Gustav, the white rat that her friend, Matilda Ward had bought her, having another human being to share her life and her home was the best thing that had happened to her in years.

Until Fred Turner came along she had forgotten how wonderful it was to hold someone else's hand. How thrilling it was to kiss and cuddle. How comforting to curl up together on the sofa with a mug of cocoa, a large glass of brandy, and the TV remote.

Sharing her bed with Fred, was nothing short of heaven. Sex with Fred might not be quite as energetic or as frequent as it had been with Hector but they were in their eighties, after all. There was something to be said for taking things slowly and gently. But they both still had a playful side.

No. Change didn't bother Hettie much at all.

Neither was it one of Fred's other suggestions. That perhaps her fondness and undeniable soft spot for Jet Cross had made her a little jealous of him marrying Mia. That was ridiculous. She couldn't be happier for them both.

Fred's final pronouncement on the matter was that perhaps she was worrying about growing too fond of Leo. And of Cathy and Daisy. In case something happened. Or in case they moved away. But it wasn't that either. Meeting Hector's illegitimate son Leo Hardman at Christmas had brought back unpleasant memories of Hector's infidelity, that was true, but getting to know Leo had given Hettie nothing but joy. Leo lived in Corner Cottage with widowed, Cathy Cole and her young daughter Daisy, and although Leo and Cathy had only met at Christmas, it was clear to

Hettie their relationship would last. Hettie was overjoyed to have them living so close. In wanting to know as much as possible about his real father Hector, Leo had spent more and more time with Hettie and Fred, and together with Cathy and Daisy, it now felt as if they were family. A real family. Which was something Hettie had always wanted, but she hadn't been able to have a child of her own.

It wasn't for want of trying. Hettie Burnstall, as she was then, had tried everything.

And then it dawned. That was it!

Hettie suddenly knew what was niggling at her.

It was Aurelia Jenkins.

Seeing her at Mia and Jet's wedding had stirred up emotions long since buried and long-forgotten memories.

Surprisingly enough, despite the fact that Hettie and Aurelia both lived in such a small village, Hettie couldn't remember the last time the pair had come face-to-face. Aurelia was the type of person who would be described as a hermit. And the only person within a sixty-mile radius about whom Hettie would never, ever gossip.

Aurelia hadn't visited The Frog and Lily in decades – until the wedding. There was no point really. The woman never touched alcohol and being a hermit, didn't particularly want to socialise, so Hettie never bumped into her there. And being a pagan, Aurelia didn't go to church.

She baked her own bread, so was never at the bakery, Lake's Bakes as it now was. But the one place she did go, was Little Pond Farm. She raised her own chickens, so she didn't need eggs, but she had always loved fresh milk, and had been getting it from the farm long before Jet had bought the place. When Sarah Cross, Jet's mum, was alive, Sarah had told Hettie that Aurelia had acquired a passion for Jet's cheese. Sarah also told her that Aurelia visited the farm around eight a.m. most days, so Hettie had always made a point of never visiting before nine.

But seeing Aurelia at the wedding was a bit of a surprise. They didn't speak of course, and the fleeting glance they exchanged was on the icy side of cool. They avoided one another at the reception, which Hettie was even more astonished to see Aurelia attending. But the woman hadn't stayed long. Just time enough to toast to Mia and Jet's happiness and then she was gone. Back to Witt's Cottage. Or Witch Cottage as some of the locals over the years had called it. But not within Aurelia Jenkins' earshot.

Even after Aurelia had left, the woman remained in Hettie's thoughts for several hours. And since the wedding, she had popped in and out of Hettie's mind from time to time. More so than Hettie would have liked.

Yes. Hettie now knew what it was that was niggling at her.

It was Aurelia Jenkins.

And as if by magic, she suddenly knew why. And exactly what she needed to do.

# Chapter Four

Tabbie was surprised by the clothes Aurelia had left on the bed for her. They weren't the rags that for some reason she had expected. They weren't drab. They weren't even that old.

Tabbie dressed quickly. She had spent longer than planned in the bath but the fragrance from Aurelia's potion had been so relaxing that she was sure she'd drifted off to sleep for a minute or two despite the dreadful storm that had momentarily raged outside. Probably not the wisest thing to do in a bath filled with water but she felt so much better for it.

The clothes on the bed smelt mildly of lavender. They'd either been washed in a scented liquid or powder, or been hanging in a wardrobe with a lavender bag or pomander. The cotton skirt and blouse were colourful and bright, but not garish, although the skirt skimmed Tabbie's ankles and was a couple of sizes too big. Aurelia had obviously thought of that because she'd also left a belt. It was long and made of twisted strands of multicoloured silk; real silk, not the faux kind. It had little charms on each end that jingled when Tabbie tied it.

At least the larger sizes meant the buttoned blouse fitted across her chest without gaping. There was also a pair of open-toed slippers with a thick band across the front. They looked brand new, which was rather surprising. Even more surprising was the fact they fitted Tabbie perfectly.

She heard voices as she made her way down the creaking stairs. One was clearly Aurelia – and she was laughing. Not the cackle Tabbie had heard earlier but a warm and friendly laugh. The other voices were male and one had a hint of a Texan drawl.

Was Aurelia married to an American? Did she have sons, perhaps? Camilla hadn't mentioned that. In fact, now that she came to think about it, Camilla hadn't told Tabbie much at all about her friend, save for the fact that they hadn't seen one another for years but despite rarely being in touch, they were still friends. Good friends.

Which was why Tabbie was here.

She pushed the door open and stepped into the hall, making her way to the kitchen from where the voices and laughter emanated. The earlier storm had abated and the entire cottage exuded an air of cosy tranquillity and warmth. Three men, one tall, muscular and blond, wearing a Stetson; one not quite as tall but slightly more agile looking with chestnut coloured hair, similar to Tabbie's and expensive-looking glasses, and one with jet black hair and a physique somewhere between his companions, stood with their backs to her. Aurelia, who was seated and facing towards the hall, spotted Tabbie immediately and beamed a welcoming smile as if it had been days, not merely an hour since they had seen one another.

'How are you feeling, Tabbie? Come and meet the boys. They've got your car out of my pond and in that sudden downpour too.'

Boys? These strapping males were hardly that, and as three pairs of eyes each scanned Tabbie from head to foot she felt the colour rise in her cheeks. Something she hadn't expected and hadn't experienced for a long time. But then she had rarely been under such scrutiny.

'Much better, thank you. I'm sorry I've been so long. Did you say they've got my car out? And during that storm? Gosh. Thanks a million times over. I really mean that.'

'It's our pleasure, ma'am,' the tall blond Texan said, removing his Stetson momentarily.

'Meet Franklin, Gill and Justin.' Aurelia pointed to each one in turn, beginning with the Texan. 'Boys. This is Tabbie, the daughter of a dear friend of mine.'

'Pleased to meet you,' the men said in unison.

'And I'm very pleased to meet you. Thank you again for saving my car.' Tabbie gave a little laugh. 'How did you manage it?'

Gill removed his glasses and wiped each lens with the tip of his shirt as he replied: 'Franklin brought a tractor, I got in the pond and tied the rope, and Justin supervised.' Putting his glasses back in place, he gave Justin a sardonic smile. Justin grabbed him by the neck in what appeared to be a wrestling hold, but both of them were laughing. Gill's jeans were sodden, so he was probably telling the truth about getting in the pond, but all three men were wet from the torrential rain.

'Someone had to,' Justin said, releasing Gill who gave him a playful shove in return.

Was that behaviour why Aurelia had called them boys?

Tabbie smiled at them. 'Well, thank you again. I'm hoping it'll start once it's had time to dry out.'

Justin shook his head. 'I wouldn't count on that.'

Not only was he extraordinarily handsome, he somehow seemed familiar.

Tabbie furrowed her brows and he clearly mistook her expression because he added: 'Sorry. But I don't think you've got a hope in hell of that happening.' He gave a light shrug and an oddly nervous smile.

'I expect you're right. Oh well. I can call the RAC and get them to tow it to a garage, I suppose. But I'll call the insurance company first and see what they suggest. I hope you don't mind me saying this, and I'm sure you've heard it hundreds of times, but you look remarkably like the Hollywood movie star, Justin Lake. You even have the same Christian name. You could earn a fortune as a celebrity double.'

The three men exchanged glances.

'Yeah. I get that a lot.' Justin emptied the contents of the cup he was holding and put it on the table. 'Thanks for the tea, Aurelia, but I think it's time I was on my way. Lovely to meet you, Tabbie. I hope you get your car sorted.'

'I'm sorry. I shouldn't have said that. It was so clichéd. I don't want to chase you away.'

He met her eyes and Tabbie's stomach gave an odd little lurch. She must be hungrier than she thought.

'You're not. I'm supposed to be meeting Bear in the pub. I hadn't realised how late it was.'

'Bear? I hope that's someone's nickname and not a real bear.' Why had she said that? What was wrong with her? She wasn't usually so socially inept? But then she didn't usually drive her car into a ditch, meet a real live witch, and end up in the company of three incredibly handsome strangers.

Justin smiled benevolently. 'Bear's a friend. His real name's Rupert. But everyone calls him Bear. Although not for the reason you might think. It's actually his middle name. Rupert Bear Day.'

'Rupert Bear Day? Gosh. I bet he was teased mercilessly at school.'

Justin winked at her. 'He still is.'

Her heart gave a little flutter. The man really was gorgeous. But then all three of them were. What were the chances of three such incredible hunks of manhood all being in one tiny village?

'Bear's the local vet,' Aurelia said. 'And a first responder. Perhaps I should've called him after your accident.'

'No, no.' Tabbie raised one hand in the air in a stop gesture. 'I'm fine.'

'It might be wise to let someone give you a once over,' Justin said.

Tabbie got the strangest feeling that Justin wasn't necessarily talking about her health. She certainly wouldn't mind him giving her a once over. Or several.

'No really, there's no need. I'm fine. Especially after the luxurious bath I've just taken. Aurelia, you should market that product. You'd make a fortune. Perhaps you do so already?'

Aurelia smiled. 'I sell it to locals. But I don't make a fortune. And neither do I want to.'

'I'd better get back,' Gill said. 'Ella will be wondering where I am. She was in the shower when Franklin called and asked me to help so I left her a note saying I was just popping out.'

He grabbed Justin's cup from the table and together with his own, placed them in the sink. Franklin handed him his, and Gill added it to the others.

'I'd best be strolling along too,' Franklin said.

Aurelia got up from her chair. 'Thank you for

your help. I knew I could count on you boys even though Jet's away.'

'You can always count on us, Aurelia, whether or not Jet's around.' Justin stepped forward and kissed Aurelia on the cheek.

'Who's Jet?'

Aurelia smiled at Tabbie. 'Jet Cross owns Little Pond Farm. It's the other side of the village. I've known him since the day he was born and a better, kinder soul you'd be hard-pressed to meet. Although he tried to hide his true nature for as long as possible. He keeps dairy cows, free range hens, and since falling in love with Mia, four reindeer.' She gave a little chuckle and shook her head. 'There's a shop on the farm and he sells milk, eggs, butter and the most delicious cheese you'll ever taste in your life. He and Mia are away on their honeymoon at the moment.'

'Mia's from the village? Sorry. I don't mean to ask so many questions. It's a habit.'

'Mia's from London, originally,' Justin said. 'She, together with her friends Ella and Ella's twin brother Garrick, moved here a little over a year ago.'

'Moved here from London? Retired here, do you mean?'

Everyone laughed except Tabbie.

Gill shook his head. 'No. Mia's in her midthirties, as are Ella and Garrick. Mia's great aunt Mattie left her Sunbeam Cottage on the condition, or so we thought, that Mia lived there for a year.

It's a long story.'

Justin slapped Gill playfully on the arm. 'And one you've partially included in the book you've written about your grandfather.'

Gill shrugged. 'That's true. But only in the epilogue explaining that Mattie continued to use her training to the full and that her activities with regards to spying overlapped into her personal life well into her nineties.'

Justin smiled at Tabbie. 'If you're interested in history, you can read all about it. Or we can fill you in on the juicy bits, if you want to leave out the boring stuff. No offence, mate.' He patted Gill on the back.

'None taken.'

'To be fair,' Justin added, 'it's far more fascinating than you might imagine.'

'It sounds intriguing. I'm definitely interested. History was one of my favourite subjects and my degree was History and English, although I later took a bit of a detour, but that's another story. Did you say spying, Gill? Is now a good time, Justin? Oh gosh no. You said you were going to the pub to meet your friend.'

'I am. But if you're interested in history, then Gill's your man.' He gave her a quick glance up and down. 'You're welcome to join us in The Frog and Lily if you fancy a drink though. And if you like rugby, you'll be in your element. Our conversation will inevitably veer in that direction, especially as I haven't been around for … That's not important. Anyway, the offer's there if you want it.'

Something was definitely not quite right with her. She was as good as throwing herself at Justin and she knew nothing about him. But he had helped rescue her car, so he wasn't a total stranger. And he was the spitting image of Justin Lake, so wasn't it understandable that her excitement was getting the better of her? It wasn't every day that she got to stand so close to such a hot guy. To three hot guys. But Justin seemed to be the one who was sending her hormones into overdrive.

Although there was something about Gill and the twinkle in his eyes when he explained who Mia was. And the way he smiled. That alone was enough to send a tingle of excitement through any female.

Perhaps she had been too long without a man in her life? She had split from her last boyfriend more than eight months ago after a short-lived relationship, and prior to that she had gone for almost a year without a significant other. Although she'd had a week-long holiday fling during that time, so it wasn't a complete year without sex. Even so, she hadn't had so much as a one-night hook up for the past eight months.

No wonder she was throwing herself at these handsome and undeniably sexy strangers; not one of whom had a wedding band on their finger. Only Gill had said he had someone to go home to. That might not necessarily be a girlfriend.

And Justin had just invited her for a drink. After the day she'd had, that might be exactly what she needed. But it would be rude to abuse Aurelia's hospitality by shooting off to the pub without first telling her why she had come to see her.

'Thank you. That's very kind. And believe me, I'd love to join you. Rugby's not my favourite topic, but red wine most certainly is. However, I've come to see Aurelia and I was supposed to be on my way back to London by now. I need to sort out my car and then I must find somewhere to stay.'

'You'll stay here,' Aurelia said, in a tone that indicated she was surprised Tabbie had thought otherwise. 'And if you want to go to the pub you're welcome to do so. Don't worry about me. I'll be here when you get back. From the looks of your car, we'll have plenty of time to talk about why you're here. I don't think you'll be going anywhere soon.'

Tabbie hesitated for a split second before shaking her head. Manners were everything and it was bad form enough to drop in on someone unexpectedly; to then leave them to enjoy oneself elsewhere was simply not cricket.

'You're all so kind. But I think it's best if I stay here and explain what prompted my unannounced arrival.'

'No problem,' Justin said. 'If you're going to be around for a day or two, one, or all of us can be found in the pub at some point most days. See you around, Tabbie.' He winked again, gave Aurelia a final little wave and left, followed directly by Gill and Franklin.

'Give me a call if you want to hear about Mattie,' Gill said, cheerfully waving a hand at Aurelia. 'Aurelia's got the number.'

'Take care now, ma'am,' Franklin added, tipping his Stetson in a respectful gesture before striding along the hall and closing the front door behind them.

'Are you sure you wouldn't rather join Justin and Bear in the pub? I meant it when I said I didn't mind.' Aurelia walked to the worktop and flicked the switch on the kettle.

Tabbie hadn't spotted the electric kettle earlier and couldn't help but smile. She had been half expecting Aurelia to boil water in the pot above the fire, but when she glanced in that direction, she saw steam rising and as she walked further into the kitchen, a delicious aroma filled her nostrils. There was something in that pot and it certainly wasn't water. Or bats or toads.

'No honestly. I'd rather stay here and chat with you. Thank you for the offer of a bed, by the way. I wasn't relishing the prospect of having to call a cab and find a hotel for the night.'

Aurelia chuckled as she placed herbs in the teapot. 'Getting a cab to come here would be nothing short of a miracle. You'd have to walk to the junction of Seaside Road and that's a fair way in the dark. And as for finding a hotel room, the nearest hotel is probably in Little Whittingdale and that's a good twenty to thirty-minute drive. Unless Justin or Jet were driving, in which case it's about fifteen.'

'I can't believe how much Justin resembles Justin Lake. Have you heard of him?'

'Justin Lake?' Aurelia chuckled softly. 'Oh yes. I've heard of Justin Lake. Bit of a one with the ladies. Although Jet was like that once, and look at him now. True Love can change a man – or a woman – in the blink of a bat's eye.'

'Jet Cross? The man who married Mia?'

'The very same.' Aurelia poured boiling water into the teapot and brought the pot, together with a cup and saucer over to the table. 'Let that stew for a minute or two. Speaking of stew, I hope you're hungry. I've made plenty. I thought the boys might want some after getting your car out of my pond, but Justin's eating at the pub with Bear, Gill's making dinner for Ella, and Franklin and Lori are off to Little Whittingdale to have dinner at the restaurant that's co-owned by Luke Martindale and that TV chef, Xavier Sombeanté.'

'Xavier Sombeanté? His restaurant's nearby? I had no idea. Gosh, today has been full of surprises.'

'You're right about that. And there's more where they came from. Which brings us back to why you're here. It suddenly occurred to me, there's nothing wrong with Cami, is there? Take a seat, dear.' She nodded towards the chair she placed in front of the fire earlier and resumed her seat close by.

'No, no,' Tabbie said, pulling her chair closer to the table before taking a seat. 'Mum's fine. Complaining about arthritis in her fingers but other than that, she's fit and healthy.'

'Arthritis, you say? I've got some herbs that'll help with that. You can pour your tea now. Supper will be ready in fifteen minutes and I'm sure I've got a bottle of wine somewhere. I can open that for you when we eat. I don't drink but I always keep a bottle handy in case anyone calls in.'

'Thank you. That's very kind. About the herbs and the wine. But please don't open a bottle just for me. I'll be fine with tea.'

'It's there to be opened. It's just a simple red. None of the fancy stuff. So you were saying, Cami's fit and healthy.'

'Yes. And she'll be sixty this year.'

'In September. The twenty-first, I believe.'

'Gosh. You remembered after all these years.'

'I never forget important things.'

Tabbie poured her tea. 'Is this lavender?'

'And honey. Always a popular choice and both from my garden.'

'You keep bees?'

'And they keep me.'

Tabbie took a sip. 'It's delicious.' She put her cup down and smiled at Aurelia. 'Mum's sixty this year, as I said, and I want to do something special for her. She's not really one for parties and although I've hinted at the idea of her going away, she's so well-travelled that I'm not sure there's anywhere she hasn't been. She also said that she'd rather stay at home and celebrate quietly. But I can't let it pass without doing something so I'm visiting all her friends, past and present – assuming they're still friends of course, but as Mum never falls out with anyone, they are. Apart from Dad. And he was never a friend, as such. But I digress. I'm asking all her friends to say a few words to her on video and I'm going to splice the clips together and make her a DVD and also keep copies in her cloud storage. Would you be happy to say a few words to her, on camera?'

'More than happy.'

'Oh no!' Tabbie leapt to her feet and headed towards the door. 'My camera's in the boot of my car. How could I have forgotten? It'll be ruined.'

'No dear. Come back and sit down. I asked the boys to retrieve your things from inside your car and from the boot. I've put your jumper, together with the clothes you were wearing, in the wash. Your bags are in my drying shed. And your camera's there too, along with some rice to help to dry it out. I believe I managed to get most of the water out. Luckily, not much water had managed to get into the boot. Probably due to the angle you went into my pond.'

'Oh gosh, thank you, Aurelia. But wasn't the car almost completely under water save for the roof?'

Aurelia smiled. 'It may have appeared so, but when the boys arrived, most of the boot was definitely above the water line. I think your camera will be almost as good as new.'

That seemed very doubtful but Tabbie didn't want to disagree. She hoped Aurelia was right. If the worst came to the worst though, she would simply have to revisit the friends she'd already filmed and ask to repeat the process with a new camera. There was no point in worrying about that now. What was done was done. Better to think about something else entirely for now.

'As I mentioned to "the boys" earlier, I'm very interested in history. I expect you've got several stories to tell, especially about your ancestor, Jennet de Witt. I'd love to hear them. Unless you'd rather not talk about her. I thought I detected a slight reluctance to elaborate and I completely understand. Our history is important to us and some people don't want to share that.'

Aurelia smiled and stood up to stir the pot above the fire with a long, wooden spoon which looked as old as Aurelia herself.

'Supper's ready.'

She walked towards the dresser and took two large bowls from the shelves and two forks and spoons from the drawer she passed on her way back to the table.

Aurelia clearly didn't want to talk about Jennet de Witt and Tabbie decided not to bring the subject up again. It would be impolite to pester, especially as a previously uninvited guest in Aurelia's house.

'Anything I can do to help?' Tabbie moved towards the pot.

'You can help yourself.' Aurelia handed her one of the bowls and smiled. 'Take as much as you want. There's plenty.'

Tabbie half-filled her bowl. 'I can always come back for more. Shall I fill your bowl too?' She placed hers on the table and reached out for the other bowl which Aurelia gave her.

'Thank you, dear,' Aurelia said, moving her chair a little closer to the table. 'Then I'll tell you a tale or two about Jennet. And about a few of my other ancestors. You may be particularly interested in my grandmother, Gosceline. She told everyone she was a white witch, and shortly after the First World War she cast a spell so that more boy babies than girls would be born here and also in the villages of Little Whitingdale, Little Stelling and Stellingfold Heights. Four out of every five babies born during the months of November, December and January each year would be male. It was because so many men from all the villages died during the war and when it ended there was a distinct shortage of males. Gosceline made sure that wouldn't happen again.'

Tabbie put Aurelia's bowl on the table in front of her and pulled her own chair to the table. It seemed Aurelia was happy to talk about Jennet and the rest of her ancestors, after all.

'Gosh. That's incredible. Do people believe the spell still works to this day?'

'All spells continue to work unless a time is placed on them to end.'

'Do you cast spells?'

'Rarely. I do get asked, from time to time, especially as we live in such troubled times, but I think of myself as semi-retired and I only cast a spell if it pleases me to do so.' She chuckled cheerfully but a moment later, a shadow seemed to fall across her eyes and her face took on a sombre expression. 'The thing is with spells and such, they don't always work out quite as one hopes. Especially if the person performing the spell makes a mistake. Even a tiny mistake can alter a spell with devastating effects. Oh gracious, don't look so concerned. I'm not talking about Gosceline, or myself for that matter. Some spells need to be cast by the person concerned. If they get it wrong and fail to follow the instructions they've been given to the letter, it can give them a result they hadn't expected.'

Aurelia coughed as if clearing something from her throat. Or an unpleasant memory of a spell gone wrong perhaps?

'Gosceline was a great … enabler,' Aurelia continued. 'One of the best. But even so, her spell changed the dynamics of the village today. There are several men born here who are now in their mid to late thirties but hardly any local women of a similar age. That meant, to even the numbers, women would have to come from outside. But Gosceline obviously thought of that because only one man born here is currently 'not spoken for' shall we say?'

'Just one?' Tabbie was disappointed.

'Yes.'

'Um. Who's that?'

Aurelia gave her a curious look as if she had something on her mind. But she smiled as she lifted a spoonful of stew towards her mouth and just before popping it in, she said: 'Justin, dear. But he says he's not staying here for long.' And she chuckled again, as she munched on her stew.

# Chapter Five

'I'm the colour of a bar of milk chocolate and it's so hot here I'd melt if it wasn't for the fact our air-conditioned villa has a private pool.' Mia smiled even though Ella was on the landline phone at Sunbeam Cottage and couldn't see her. 'Not that we really need a pool. We've got access to a private beach which is about a minute's stroll away past a couple of coconut-laden palm trees.'

'It sounds horrendous.'

Mia gave a little laugh. 'The journey *was* pretty horrendous. Well, not horrendous exactly. Travelling First Class is anything but that, but it was long. Really long. Thirty-three hours, door-to-door.'

'Crickey! I still don't know why you and Jet wanted to travel nine and a half thousand miles to some private island in the middle of the Pacific for your honeymoon when Little Pondale has a perfectly good beach, and the village green is sort of like an island. Only greener. With a pond.'

'Yeah right.'

'Did it honestly take that long? Did you and Jet join the mile-high club? First Class has beds, doesn't it?'

Mia tutted good-naturedly. 'Yes, it took that long. Yes, there were beds. And no, we didn't. We didn't even have sex the night we arrived. We were both too tired. After the flight to Los Angeles we had a four-hour stopover, followed by a connecting flight from Tahiti to Bora Bora and then another flight to here. When they said we'd be travelling by Twin Otter, I half expected to see two of the furry creatures strapped together like the out-rigger canoes we spotted in Tahiti, until Jet told me it was an aircraft. But being in a small plane certainly gives you a spectacularly stunning view. And we made up for the missed sex the following morning.'

Mia had read that the flight over Bora Bora gave visitors one of the most beautiful vistas in the world, and it hadn't disappointed, but the final twenty-minute flight to Tetiaroa, the private island and home of the luxury eco-resort, The Brando, was something else. Looking down over the atoll into glistening, pristine waters, several differing shades of blue where manta rays, dolphins and flying fish, together with black-tipped reef sharks glided serenely amongst the coral, took Mia's breath away. No wonder the island's former owner, Hollywood legend, Marlon Brando after whom The Brando was named, fell in love with the place when he was filming *Mutiny on the Bounty* all those years ago.

'I bet you're missing Little Pondale no end. Although, we've had rain and storms and all sorts of peculiar weather since the day you left and it's been bloody chilly for June.'

'Funnily enough, I am. Just a bit. Not the rain though. Mainly missing you, and Mum, and everyone. But not enough to want to come home yet. Two more glorious weeks of spending my days basking in the sun, swimming in an impossibly clear, blue ocean surrounded by icing-sugar-white sand and gently swaying palms, and my nights in the arms of the sexiest, most gorgeous man alive. I can't believe I got this lucky.'

'I can't believe you got him to agree to leave his beloved farm for a month. If anyone ever doubted how much Jet Cross loves you, that alone should set them straight.'

'He tells me he's not missing it much at all, but I know for a fact he called Franklin two days after we arrived. But to be fair, I did ask him to. Justin's great and I know he's been Jet's best friend for ever and ever, but I was a bit worried about leaving him in charge of Little M, let alone helping out with a herd of cows, four reindeer and a barnful of chickens. Especially now he's a Hollywood film star.'

Ella coughed lightly. 'Yeah. You could've slapped my face with a wet kipper when I heard he was staying for the duration of your honeymoon.

What is that about? Someone said all the media coverage and paparazzi intrusion gets on his nerves, but it sort of goes with the territory of fame and fortune and he signed up for that. Has Jet said anything about why Justin wanted to stay on?'

'Nope. I know as much as you. Justin asked Jet shortly before our wedding if he could stay at the farmhouse while we were away, and as it saved Mum looking after Little M, and meant an extra hand to replace Jet on the farm, it seemed like a no-brainer. Jet says Justin merely wants a break from the bright lights and non-stop partying.'

'There's no better place to get away from all that stuff than Little Pondale.' Ella laughed but only for a second, her voice taking on a serious, almost melancholy tone. 'It's still weird each time I bump into him. I thought Gill might be jealous, but he's not.'

'Oh? Does he have anything to be jealous about? You got over Justin a long time ago, didn't you? You were even the one who broke it off, really, although I know Justin was leaving in any event.'

'Yeah. But Justin looks twice as gorgeous now than he did when we were dating. Or perhaps it's the fame and fortune that make him more attractive. I don't know. But I can't help wondering whether we'd get back together – even for just a fling – if I wasn't with Gill. I'm not saying I want a fling with Justin. I love Gill, don't get me wrong. It's just that … well … I'm not sure about the future.'

Mia sat upright and swung her legs over the side of the sun lounger, burying her toes in the soft white sand. 'The future with Gill, you mean? Are you having doubts about him? I thought you two were for life.'

'So did I. But shortly after we waved you and Jet off, I made a joke about how lucky you two were to be spending a month on a private island in the middle of the Pacific Ocean and that he and I would be lucky to have a honeymoon in Margate, and he went all weird on me.'

'All weird? How?' Mia took the rainbow-coloured cocktail the personal butler had brought her on a tray, and smiled at him before returning her attention back to Ella.

'He sort of coughed and the colour drained from his face. Then he fiddled with his glasses, like he does when he's troubled by something, and he asked me why I'd said that. I told him it was a joke and he frowned and coughed again and said: "Oh okay." And he sounded relieved, Mia. As if the thought of us getting married was upsetting to say the least. Every time I mention your wedding, or your honeymoon or stuff, he changes the subject. Bree and Garrick had dinner with us the other night and Bree asked me to help her with her own wedding – which was bloody strange because she's the wedding planner, not me, and she's got three assistants now, but anyway – Gill paled immediately and when Bree asked if she should save a date for a certain other couple's wedding, Gill said that he didn't know of anyone else in the village who had any plans to get married.'

'Hmm. That *is* weird. Perhaps he's nervous about it. But you've only been together since last October so there's no rush, is there?'

Ella tutted loudly. 'Says the woman who's just married the man she started dating … last October.'

'Point taken. But I'd known Jet since May.'

'Ah yes. Four months makes such a huge difference.'

'Okay, okay.' Mia sipped her cocktail. 'Oh my God. I wish you were here, Ella. This cocktail is orgasmic. You'd love it.'

'I wish I were there too. Although Jet might not be so pleased to see me. Where is he anyway?'

'He's taking a shower before lunch.'

'And you're not in there with him? Has the passion cooled now you're married?' Ella laughed.

'If anything, it's increased. Which I didn't think was possible. But I wanted to call you because I keep forgetting you're eleven hours ahead and if I hadn't called now it'd be another day until we talked.'

Ella yawned, as if to emphasize the fact that it was eleven p.m. in Little Pondale. 'Yeah. I was beginning to think you'd forgotten your best friend. We've never gone so long without speaking every day. I'm just glad you've found the time amongst your non-stop schedule of sun, sea and sex to phone me.'

'Sun, sea, sex and alcohol. Actually, there's quite a bit to do here. Tetiaroa may be small but The Brando has thirty-five villas, so we're not completely alone even though we hardly ever see anyone. There're two gourmet restaurants, two bars, a fitness centre, swimming pool, library, tennis court, a boutique, and an out of this world spa that's built over a freshwater pond. Not to mention a shop that sells beautiful jewellery made from exquisite black pearls, one or two items of which I may or may not be bringing back with me for a certain best friend.'

'Black pearls? Oh Mia. I'll love you forever if you do.'

'You'll love me forever even if I don't. But I will. Anyway, apart from all the swimming, sunbathing and spa treatments, we've taken excursions to other islands – all of which are miles away. We've been to Bora Bora and yesterday to Tahiti. We didn't get time to see much of either of them between flights so it was great to do both. Bora Bora's beautiful but so is Tahiti – and it's larger so there's more to do. The Botanical Gardens make my garden look pathetic. The Gauguin Museum's small but interesting. Like me.' Mia gave a little laugh and took a sip of her cocktail.

'Who told you that?' Ella laughed too.

'Shut up. Where was I? Oh yes. We went to Point Venus and saw the Monument Tower, which was built in honour of Captain Cook, and the Bounty Memorial in memory of the HMS *Bounty*. I've learnt so much. It was actually quite humbling to think those famous captains – Samuel Wallis, James Cook and William Bligh had all stood where I was standing, or thereabouts, in the 1700s.'

'Didn't the locals murder Captain Cook? No wait. That was on Hawaii, not Tahiti. Sea captains are not my *Mastermind* subject of choice. But as an editor, writers are. Several famous writers spent time in Tahiti you know. Robert Louis Stevenson lived there. W. Somerset Maugham wrote *The Moon and Sixpence*, which I'm sure was loosely based on Gauguin's life when he lived there. But he was an artist. Who else? Ah, Herman Melville, Charles Nordhoff and James Norman Hall. Jack London travelled there aboard the Snark.'

'Yes. We heard a bit about all of them. And it took them a lot longer than thirty-three hours to get here. I don't envy them their journeys.'

'Ooh! And did they mention Rupert Brooke? I'm sure they did. He's supposed to have found true love there but I'm not sure how *true* that love was. He left his Tahitian lover when he returned to England. The git. I wonder if Gill's love for me is that kind of True Love. I'm telling you now, Mia, if the little sod leaves me, I'll never love again. And nor will he. Because I'll throttle him.'

'I'm sure Gill has no intention of leaving you, so stop worrying.'

'That's easy for you to say. Only a couple of hours ago he came home and talked virtually non-stop about some woman called Tabbie who'd driven her car into Aurelia Jenkins' pond.'

'What? I bet Aurelia wasn't pleased about that. Was anyone hurt?'

'Apparently not. Franklin, Justin and Gill had to go and help get it out though and when Gill came home it was all "Tabbie this and Tabbie that". And that's another thing. I thought he'd only met Aurelia once but he says he's seen her a few times.'

'Does that matter? You don't tell him how often you bump into everyone, do you? But what else did he say about this Tabbie? What was she doing near the pond in the first place? Witt's Cottage is a bit off the beaten track. To end up in the pond means either this Tabbie was dreadfully lost or–'

'She was going to see Aurelia. Her mum's a friend of Aurelia's apparently. Anyway, you don't want to hear about all that now. I'll email you. It'll give you something to read while you're lounging in the sun.'

'Okay, but make sure you do. And don't leave out any details.'

'I'll be sure to tell you everything. It'll be like reading a novel.' Ella gave a wistful sigh. 'What else have you been doing?'

'Lots. I thought we'd be lounging on the beach all day but no. And having beaten my fear of water, last year, it nearly came back. We only went swimming with sharks the other day. Sharks, Ella! Can you believe it? Okay, they were small sharks. About five feet or so, and the guy who took us assured us they only take a bite out of a human as a last resort, but still. I've never been so scared in my life, but I was determined to do it. Jet said I could stay in the out-rigger canoe if I wanted, but it was a sweltering day and the water looked so cool and inviting. Even with the sharks. Jet stayed by my side the entire time and said that if a shark tried to attack, he'd make sure it got him and not me.'

'Now that is True Love.' Ella let out an even bigger sigh than before.

Mia sighed too. 'I know. I'm so lucky. Oh, and we visited both a banana and a vanilla plantation. Jet loved those, as you can imagine, being a farmer. One day next week we're going to a place that grows pineapples, avocados and the infamous breadfruit, too. And I wish I could grow some of the flowers I've seen. The bougainvillaea, passion flower, hibiscus and frangipani are intoxicating but the Tiare, which is Tahiti's national flower has an unbelievably heavenly fragrance, and it's got a star-shaped bloom which is stunning. I hate to admit this, but I've been wearing flowers in my hair since the day we arrived. You have to be careful which side you wear it, you know. The left side means you're taken and the right side means you're available. I had no idea until one of the wonderful staff told me. That could've been embarrassing otherwise. And I've learnt how to do the Ori Tahiti. That's the traditional dance. It's like the Hula. It's incredible. Jet says it's really sexy, so naturally I've been trying to perfect it. My hips and knees are killing me. I wish you'd been here having lessons too. We'd have been rolling on the floor laughing.'

'I miss you so much, Mia. But it sounds like you're having a fantastic time. And you deserve it. All your dreams have come true, haven't they?'

'Yep. As I keep saying, I'm very, very lucky.'

There it was again. That tiny pin-prick-sized pain in her heart. It happened every time she said those words. Why was that?

Was it because although she had no right to ask for more than she'd already got, there was one more thing she wanted to make her happiness complete?

A child.

It was early days and she and Jet had plenty of time but she couldn't help wondering if it would happen. She hadn't told Jet of her concerns. He would say she was being silly – and she probably was. But something had been bugging her ever since Bree had broken the news that she and Garrick were expecting.

The fortune-teller at the Summer Fête last August had been proved right, once again.

And that was the problem. Because

everything the fortune-teller had told Mia, had also come true. But one thing the fortune-teller hadn't told her was that she would have children.

Did that mean she wouldn't?

'Are you still on the phone with your mum. Or is this Ella?' Jet sauntered towards her wearing smart black trousers and a pale blue shirt, highlighting his bronzed, beautiful body where the skin was revealed. He also wore that grin on his face that had made her heart skip a beat every time she saw it, long before she had realised she had fallen in love with him.

She smiled, the little hole in her heart forgotten as an arid breeze lifted strands of his hair, still the colour of midnight even in the blinding sunshine, and he reached out his hand towards her.

'Yes,' she said, almost sighing the words out. 'It's Ella.'

Jet closed the gap between him and Mia and wrapped one arm around her waist. 'Hello, Ella. We love you. We miss you. But we're going to say goodbye for now because I'm ravenous. And I don't just mean for lunch. It's been at least an hour since I kissed my wife.'

# Chapter Six

'You must've seen her at the wedding,' Ella said, pointing at a large coffee-iced cream bun, a jam and cream doughnut and a sugar-coated apple and cream turnover in the display cabinet in Lake's Bakes the following day. 'She looked like she wouldn't be out of place teaching at *Hogwarts*.'

Jenny Lake shoved a wayward strand of wild red hair back behind the white cotton headband she was wearing and tightened the additional band holding her ponytail in place. She knit her brows as she grabbed a box from a stack to the right of her and a large flat cake knife from the top of the counter. She slid the flat of the knife beneath the turnover and lifted the cake towards the box, stopping suddenly. 'Oh wait.' Knife and turnover hovered above the box. 'Was she the woman dressed head to toe in purple? I think she even had a purple cloak.'

Ella nodded. 'Yep. That was her. I'd only met her once before, myself, and that was very briefly at Christmas. Massive hermit, apparently. But Jet told me – well, he told Mia and Mia told me – that he's known her all his life and sees her a lot because she goes to the farm shop for milk and she's addicted to his cheese. But then, who isn't?'

'Not such a massive hermit then? Just antisocial perhaps?' Jenny popped the turnover in the box and reached for the cream bun.

'Well, she definitely doesn't like Hettie. And I think that feeling is mutual. I saw them glaring at one another a couple of times at the reception but when I asked Hettie about it a couple of days later, she immediately changed the subject. Obviously that didn't stop me. But eventually all she said was, "I'd rather not discuss Mrs Jenkins, deary. And you'd be wise to do likewise." Or something along those lines. Which naturally made me even more curious.'

Jenny laughed, adding the bun to the box and leaning further into the cabinet for the doughnut. 'I thought hell would freeze over before I saw the day when Hettie didn't want to talk about someone. So did you find out anything?' She made room for the doughnut and closed the lid of the box.

Ella shook her head and sighed. 'Nope. Hettie's not the only one who didn't want to discuss Aurelia Jenkins.' She leant forward, crossing her arms and resting them on the glass cover of the cabinet, above the large display of Jenny's delicious cakes. 'You know that horror story about some guy whose name you mustn't say because if you do, he'll appear and kill you, or whatever?'

Jenny looked thoughtful but slowly shook her head. 'No. But then I'm not really a fan of horror stories. If I watch a horror film I have nightmares for weeks afterwards.'

'I don't particularly like them myself. My uncle's a big fan though and I remember seeing this film when I stayed with him early last year. Just before we moved here, in fact. But I can't for the life of me remember what it's called. Anyway. The point I'm making is that it seems to be a bit like that with Aurelia Jenkins. Everyone's too scared to say her name in case she appears and does them in. Or puts a spell on them, or something.'

Jenny raised her brows. 'So the woman really is a witch then? But how do you know that? I thought you said you didn't find out anything about her.'

'I didn't. It was Gill who told me last night. And that's also weird. As I told Mia last night, I didn't even know he knew Aurelia Jenkins but he told me he's met her several times and not just at the wedding. He also said that she was apparently a good friend of Mattie's.' Ella stood upright and took the box Jenny handed her, slipping it into the tote bag she'd brought with her.

'Mattie's? Mia's great aunt? Wow!'

Ella grinned. 'Is there another Mattie? But what I also don't get is that if Mattie was friends with a witch, why did she go to so much trouble to get Mia and Jet together when she could've simply asked her friend, Aurelia to cast a spell on them.'

'Perhaps she wanted them to meet and fall in love the 'normal' way.'

Ella tutted. 'There was nothing 'normal' in the way she got them to meet. And what also gets me is why Hettie's never mentioned the woman. She's the one who told us about all the old myths, legends and superstitions in this village. But did she ever mention that there's a bona fide witch on our doorstep? Nope.'

'Wasn't she the one who told Mia about the witch who cast a spell so that more male babies than females were born around here?'

'I don't think so, no. No. I'm pretty sure that was Anna. One of the women Mia met on the beach. Anna said that her grandmother talked about Gosceline, and she told Mia about the spell, but no one actually mentioned that the witch had lived in this village or that her descendants were still here.'

'I wasn't sure I really believed the story about that spell. Although there certainly are more men than women around these parts. But wasn't Gosceline a white witch? White witches only do good things, don't they? So why would people be afraid to mention Aurelia's name?'

Ella frowned. Jenny had a point. Why would people be afraid? 'No idea.'

Jenny looked perplexed. 'Perhaps Hettie's the only one who still believes in all that stuff. Maybe the rest have simply forgotten it all. Or dismissed it as mumbo-jumbo. That's the reason why no one talks about Aurelia. And if she likes her privacy, perhaps everyone merely respects that.'

'I don't think that would stop Hettie from gossiping about her. No, there's something odd about Aurelia Jenkins. I'm sure of it. And not everyone thinks all that stuff is nonsense. You believe in The Wishing Tree, don't you?'

Jenny nodded a little reluctantly.

'Then there's the Whispering Cave and skinny-dipping in the pond at Frog's Hollow. And let's not forget the fortune-teller who comes here every year. The one who told our fortunes at the Summer Fête last year. But that was before you arrived. Anyway. What I'm saying is this place is surrounded by that sort of magical, mystical stuff and as crazy as it sounds, some of it seems to work. So when I think about it. Why would a witch living in this village come as a surprise to anybody? Including me.'

'When you put it like that ...' Jenny pulled a face. 'Which reminds me. Are you going skinny-dipping this year? You said you went last year, didn't you?'

Ella nodded. 'For all the good it did me. Although it did bring Lori and Franklin together.

Mia wasn't there of course, because she hadn't beaten her fear of water at the time and she didn't want to merely stand and watch. And she and Jet won't be back in time for this year.' She shrugged. 'The thing is, Gill's not keen on the idea. He can be such a prude at times.'

'Glen's definitely not going. Not because he's a prude but because he doesn't think the local vicar should be seen running around naked at what is essentially a pagan event. He says it's entirely up to me whether I go or not, but I don't think I want to. Not without him.'

Ella pouted. 'That's how I feel. I'm not sure I want to go without Gill. And Cathy told me the other day when we were discussing it, that she doesn't want to go without Leo, who'll be in London, because it's a Monday. And that's the other thing.' She leant forward and whispered, 'The curse of Frog's Hollow.'

Jenny's anxious expression faded as quickly as it appeared. 'But didn't Hettie say that if Midsummer's Night falls on a Monday it's still safe to go to the pond because on that special night Frog's Hollow is protected from the curse?'

'Yeah. But I'm not certain I want to take Hettie's word for it. Are you?'

Jenny looked doubtful. 'No. So that's definitely made up my mind. I'm not going.'

Ella took a deep breath. 'I'm not going either.'

Jenny grinned. 'So … what else did Gill say about Aurelia Jenkins?'

Ella frowned. 'He, like everyone else, didn't seem to want to talk about Aurelia either. The only thing he did seem to want to talk about was this Tabbie woman.'

'Oh?'

Ella pulled a face and changed her tone to mimic Gill. 'She's terribly well-spoken. And terribly well-educated. And terribly attractive. And terribly interested in history – which as we all know, just happens to be one of my favourite subjects. And she's terribly nice.'

Jenny raised her brows and sniggered. 'She sounds … terrible. You've got Gill's voice down to a tee but he didn't really say it like that, did he?'

Ella smirked. 'Nah. When I asked him where the hell he'd been because his note said he was just popping out and he was gone for over an hour, all he said was that Aurelia had a visitor who'd driven her car into Aurelia's pond and that Franklin had called and asked him to give them a hand. Franklin and Justin, that is. To get the car out of the pond. Then he'd had a cup of tea – despite the fact that he was soaked – and that he'd told Tabbie, the visitor, to phone if she wanted to chat about Mattie or anything else.'

'Er. So where did you get all that other stuff from? About her being well-educated and such. Or did you just make that up?'

'Oh no. He did tell me all that. Sort of. When I asked him about it.'

Jenny tilted her head to one side. 'Asked? Or interrogated?'

Ella grinned. 'You know me so well. If I'd had a rack to hand, he'd have been stretched to within an inch of his life. It was like he didn't want to talk about her. And you know what that means, don't you?'

'Do I?' Jenny looked unsure.

Ella tutted. 'It means he was attracted to her.'

'Oh come on.' Now Jenny tutted too. 'It means nothing of the sort. And you've just said yourself that he didn't want to talk about Aurelia either. So on that basis, he must be attracted to Aurelia as well.'

'Aurelia's in her sixties – and looks twice as old as that.'

'Whatever floats Gill's boat.' Jenny laughed and shook her head. 'You're being ridiculous, Ella, if you don't mind me saying so. Gill adores you, you know that.'

'Does he? I thought he did but now I'm not so sure.'

Jenny reached out across the counter and poked Ella's shoulder with her fingertip.

'Is something going on that I don't know about? Ever since the wedding you've seemed … I don't know. Not quite your usual happy, carefree self. Are you having doubts about your relationship with Gill? I thought you two were for ever.'

Ella snorted. 'That's exactly what Mia said.' She looked Jenny in the eye. 'And it's what I thought too, but recently … well, since the wedding really … things haven't been going quite so well.'

'In what way?'

Ella shrugged. 'I don't really know. He seems a bit … distant. You know what it's like when you've got to tell someone something but you don't want to because you know they're not going to like it and so you keep putting it off?'

'Um. No. But I think I understand what you mean.'

'Well. I think Gill's got something to tell me – only he's not. Because he knows I won't like it.'

'But that can't have anything to do with this … Tabbie, can it? He only met her last night.'

Ella shook her head. 'No. I think it has something to do with me. I think … I think he might be going off me.'

Jenny gave a burst of laughter. 'Now that really is ridiculous, Ella. I'm sure you're wrong. Perhaps he's just worried about his book, or something else he's working on. Or something completely unrelated. Wait. Didn't you date my cousin last year? Maybe Gill's jealous. Perhaps he's worried that you might decide you'd rather get back with Justin than be with Gill. Have you thought about that?'

'Actually I have. I've thought about it quite a lot. But Justin's famous now and really it was just about the sex with him and me, so it wouldn't work. Besides, he'll be going back to L.A very soon and there's no way I'm ever leaving Little Pondale. And I never thought I'd hear myself say that this time last year.'

Jenny looked confused and then she tutted and sighed. Leaning forward, she poked Ella's shoulder once again.

'I didn't mean, have you thought about going back out with Justin, you twit. I meant, have you thought that Gill might think you want to do that? That you might be considering dumping him to date my cousin again.'

'Oh right. Um. Yes. I did wonder if he'd think that. But he doesn't seem the least bit bothered about Justin being here. He didn't even mind when Justin asked me to dance at the wedding. And when I told him that Justin was staying on for the entire month that Mia and Jet are away, he simply said, "Yes. So I heard." Then he smiled and changed the subject as if we were discussing the weather, not the fact that one of the hottest men I've ever had sex with, not to mention, one of the best-looking ones, was going to be hanging around for four weeks.'

'That just proves Gill trusts you.'

'Or that he couldn't care less if I ran away with a Hollywood heartthrob. I think he'd be more concerned if I ran off with one of his bloody history books that he uses for research.'

'Oh, Ella. You–'

'Coo-ey!'

Whatever Jenny was about to say was cut short by Hettie who pushed the door open and stood beside Ella, beaming.

'Just the person I wanted to see, deary. And hello to you too, Jenny dear.' She nodded her head at Jenny before turning her full attention back to Ella. 'Gill's good at digging things up, isn't he?'

Ella exchanged surprised glances with Jenny.

'Um. Not really, no. Garrick's probably more your man for that.'

'Garrick? I didn't know he was interested in that sort of thing.'

'He's not. Especially. But he's better suited to it than Gill.'

'Are you sure, deary? I thought Gill was the one who helped find Mattie's diaries?'

'He was. But we didn't dig them up. They were hidden in the attic. Beneath the window seat. Gill just showed us where the lock contraption was hidden.'

'Precisely, deary. And he knew that because he's so good at digging things up.'

Ella scratched her forehead with her free hand. 'Um. Okay. Whatever. What do you want Gill to dig up, Hettie – and why are you asking me? Why don't you just ask him yourself?'

'I was going to, deary. But he said he was in a hurry and had to dash out, and that you were in Lake's Bakes.'

'Okay. Now I'm utterly confused,' Ella said with a slightly irritated sigh. 'I don't know why Gill said that because Bree's coming round for afternoon tea. I've just got cakes. Sometimes I think we're becoming so provincial.' She rolled her eyes and smirked at Jenny. 'So he wouldn't be dashing out anywhere. But anyway. Tell me what you want him to dig up and I'll pass the message on. I think he's got some wellies somewhere. But I don't think he'll want to be in your garden today because rain's forecast again this afternoon. Torrential, so they say.'

'And it's none of my concern, Hettie,' Jenny put in. 'But after all the rain we've had this week already, your garden's going to be like a quagmire. Not the best time to dig something up. Better to wait until the ground's a little drier. Mud's much heavier to lift.'

Hettie looked from Ella to Jenny and back again with an expression of utter confusion on her face.

'Why are you two talking about my garden and wellies, my dears? What have wellies got to do with anything? Or the weather. I don't expect him to sit outside.'

'But I thought you wanted him to dig something up?' Ella glanced at Jenny who shrugged and shook her head.

'I do, deary. Fred's been trying, bless him. He's usually very good, but this has got him stumped. He was the one who suggested Gill. And it makes perfect sense.'

'Not to me it doesn't,' Ella said, somewhat sarcastically.

'Oh?' Hettie gave her a look of mild disbelief. 'After everything he dug up about his grandfather and Mattie, I'm surprised to hear you say that. If anyone can dig up a map of Little Pondale from the 1600s, Fred and I were both certain it would be Gill. If only he hadn't had to dash off to see a cat.'

'A map!' Jenny laughed. 'You want Gill to do research. That kind of 'digging up'. We thought–'

'A cat?' Ella queried. 'Gill told you he was dashing off to see a cat?'

Hettie, now looking even more confused, nodded and smiled. 'Yes, deary. I said I wanted to ask a favour and he said it would either have to wait until he got back, or that I could ask you, and that you were in Lake's Bakes because he was dashing off to see a tabby and really couldn't stop to chat. Are you thinking of getting a cat, deary? I'd best not tell Prince Gustav. He's not terribly fond of cats.'

'Prince Gustav isn't the only one.' Ella shot a look at Jenny. 'I'm not terribly fond of a certain *Tabbie*, either.'

# Chapter Seven

Tabbie smiled at Gill as he approached the bar in The Frog and Lily, where she was perched on a stool, sipping a glass of wine.

Gill smiled back, removing his glasses as he reached her side, and wiping them with a cloth he had taken from the pocket of his jeans. He put his glasses back in place and nodded at the beautiful redhead who had just served Tabbie and was now serving someone else further along the bar.

'Thank you for meeting me,' Tabbie said. 'I hope you didn't mind me calling, but you did say yesterday that if I wanted to ask you any questions, I could. Are you sure you didn't have plans this afternoon?'

'Nothing that couldn't wait. I'm glad you called. It's nice to see you again. What's happened with your car?'

Tabbie glanced up to the heavens. 'Oh gosh. Don't get me started on that subject. Are all the people who work at insurance companies trained to be annoying, or is it just in their nature? Sorry. That was mean. Let's just say, the matter is in hand and leave it at that.' She laughed as the beautiful barmaid sauntered towards them. 'Let me buy you a drink.'

'Hello, Gill,' the barmaid said, giving Tabbie a sideways glance. 'What can I get you? Is Ella on her way?'

'Hi, Alexia. I'll have a pint of lager please, and no, Ella's not joining us. I suspect she'll be talking to Hettie for at least the next half hour and Bree's going round for tea. Have you two met?'

Alexia grinned. 'Me and Bree? Or do you mean me and your new friend? In which case, no.'

Gill sighed softly as if he had heard that quip, or something similar, several times.

'Tabbie, this is Alexia Bywater. Her parents, Alec and Freda own this pub. Alexia meet Tabbie … I'm sorry, Tabbie. I don't know your surname.'

'Talbaine. I'm Tabbie Talbaine.'

'Of course you are,' Alexia said, somewhat facetiously, but she threw Tabbie a brief smile.

'Tabbie's staying with Aurelia,' Gill continued.

Alexia looked stunned. 'Aurelia? Aurelia Jenkins? How do you know Aurelia? She never has visitors.'

Tabbie ignored the inquisitorial stare, and smiled. 'Aurelia and my mother are friends. I hadn't planned to stay but unfortunately, I had a little accident and my car was towed to a garage this morning. It's going to take a day or so to sort out a replacement, apparently.'

'Oh, you're the one who drove into Aurelia's pond last night.' Alexia poured Gill's lager and put the pint glass in front of him on the bar.

Tabbie coughed. 'Word travels fast in this village.'

Alexia shrugged. 'I heard Bear talking to Aurelia on the phone this morning, and afterwards, he told me what had happened. Aurelia wanted him to pop round and take a quick look at you sometime today.'

Tabbie tutted. 'There's really no need. I told Aurelia I'm perfectly fine. I hadn't realised she had made that call.'

'Maybe she's worried you'll sue her. People do that. They have an accident and then blame someone else for it happening.'

'I will do no such thing, and I'm sure Aurelia knows that.'

Tabbie held a £10 note out to Alexia who took it, smiled mischievously, and handed back some change.

'No need to bite my head off. I'm only saying.'

Alexia leant her elbows on the bar as if waiting to join in with Tabbie and Gill's conversation.

'Perhaps we'd be more comfortable at a table,' Gill said, giving Alexia a look of mild reprimand.

'Don't mind me.' Alexia straightened up. 'I can take a hint. Excuse me. I've got customers to serve. Enjoy your drinks. And say hello to Ella for me, Gill.'

Tabbie watched her sashay away.

'Have I caused some sort of situation? She seemed less than happy to find you here with me, which is rather odd, as she doesn't know me at all.'

'Don't worry about it. It's just 'small village mentality'. In a good way. It's a very close-knit community and as in all small villages I should imagine, people look out for one another. Although that wasn't always the case here. But that's another story. Alexia and my girlfriend, Ella are friends. It's no big deal. I'll explain to Ella later.'

'Do you need to explain? Sorry. That sounded rude. What I meant was, there isn't anything to explain. I just wanted to ask you a couple of questions about the village, that's all. It's not as though this is a date or anything.'

Tabbie laughed, but Alexia had made her uncomfortable. Didn't Gill's girlfriend trust him? Did she have reason not to? Did Gill think Tabbie's call was an excuse to see him again? No. Alexia's behaviour was making her overthink things.

'I know,' Gill said, but he looked a little disappointed when he smiled. 'Let's grab a table anyway or Alexia will spend the entire time eavesdropping. There's one free over by the window.' He nodded in that direction.

Tabbie slid down from the stool and as Gill stood to one side, led the way to the table Gill had pointed out.

'What did you want to ask me?' Gill said, the second he sat down.

Tabbie took a swig of wine and, after placing her glass on the table, a deep breath. She leant forward and stared at her hands. This was going to sound silly – unless Gill believed Aurelia Jenkins really was a witch.

# Chapter Eight

Bree glanced at her watch for the umpteenth time. Where on earth was Ella? They were supposed to be having tea this afternoon, and discussing how Ella could help with the wedding.

Bree smiled, despite being irritated.

Her wedding. Her very own wedding. Something she had begun to think would never happen. If anyone had told her, just a few months ago, that Bree Wright would be getting married this October, she would've told them they were delusional.

Yet here she was, waiting for her future sister-in-law to discuss that very thing. And she wasn't only getting married. She was pregnant too. With twins. So next year was going to be even more amazing. They were due at the end of February. The twenty-seventh, if her timing was correct.

Sometimes, she still woke up in the night and half expected to be in a single bed in a tiny room in a shared house in London. And still single.

Working in Sainsbury's with only foolish and impossible dreams of having her own business.

Not that her dreams had proved to be impossible. They had turned into reality. And then a miracle had happened. No. Not just one miracle but two. She had seen the love of her life once more, and this time, he'd seen her. Really seen her. And fallen in love with her. And shown her how much he loved her and wanted her. Then the second miracle – she had fallen pregnant and in doing so, had proved that doctors don't always know everything.

Which was both a good thing and a bad. If a doctor could be wrong about her chances of ever becoming a mother, they could also be wrong when they told her that everything was going well and that she and both the babies were fine.

What if they were wrong about that? What if the babies weren't developing as they should? What if she was doing something wrong? What if her morning sickness wasn't just the usual everyday nausea that lots of women felt? What if–

'Sorry. Sorry. Sorry.' Ella rushed towards her, panting and red-faced. She placed a hand on her chest and bent over, gasping for breath.

'Oh my God, Ella! Are you okay?'

Ella straightened up, her hand still on her chest. 'Do I look okay?'

Bree hesitated for a second. 'Frankly, no. It's not your heart, is it?'

'Yes. But not in the way you mean. I'm not having a heart attack or anything. It's just breaking in two, that's all.'

'Why? What's happened?' Bree reached out and slid an arm across Ella's shoulders.

'Gill's in the pub with a strange woman. I've just peered in the window and they're deep in conversation.'

'Strange in what way? Didn't he tell you he was meeting someone? It's probably in connection with his book or something. But if you're concerned, why didn't you simply go in and ask him who she is?'

'I know who she is. She's the woman who drove her car into Aurelia Jenkins' pond last night.'

'Oh yes. I heard about that from Lori this morning. Franklin told her they had to use a tractor to get it out. It's probably a write-off. And even if it's not, would anyone want to sit in a car that's been in a muddy pond? I know I wouldn't.'

Ella frowned. 'I don't care about her bloody car, Bree. What I want to know is why he's meeting her. I have my suspicions of course, but I don't want him to think I'm jealous.'

'But clearly you are.'

'Yes. Thank you for stating the obvious. I know that and you know that, but he doesn't need to know that too.' Ella stared at Bree's large baby bump. 'Why are you standing out here anyway?'

'I was waiting for you. We were supposed to be having tea, remember? And discussing my wedding.'

'I remember. Why d'you think I ran all the way from the pub. Nearly killing myself in the process, I might add. And why d'you think I got these cakes?' Ella held up her handbag. 'Ah. Um. I must've left the cakes and my tote bag at Jenny's. Go inside and make yourself comfortable and I'll nip back and get them.'

'I didn't bring Garrick's key,' Bree yelled after Ella's retreating back. 'That's why I was outside.'

Ella spun round but continued running, only backwards. 'You don't need it. The door's unlocked. It always is.' She grinned and spun round to face in the direction of Lake's Bakes.

Bree sighed and shook her head. Typical Ella. And fancy shouting out for everyone to hear that she always leaves the door unlocked. Bree glanced up and down Lily Pond Lane. Apart from her and Ella, there wasn't another soul in sight.

Oh well. This was Little Pondale, after all. Everyone left their front doors unlocked around here. Everyone except Bree. She still hadn't got used to that, and Willow Cottage had the bolt slid across the door every single night. Unless Garrick was staying over, in which case he was the one who locked up. Or probably, didn't.

She opened the door to Sunbeam Cottage and walked into the bright and sunny hall leading into the kitchen beyond. She could feel the breeze in her face. Ella had obviously left the back door to the garden open too. Bearing in mind there was a public beach beyond the garden, that wasn't a sensible thing to do. But once again, Bree reminded herself, this was Little Pondale, not London.

She carefully deposited her laptop bag on a chair at the table. The bag was a gift from Garrick and the laptop inside was another gift from Mia and Jet to give both her and her then fledgling business a boost, and she was determined to look after both gifts. Not only because the bag and the laptop were from people she loved, but also because the laptop was very expensive and she wasn't yet used to owning such expensive items.

She switched the kettle on and took a seat next to her bag.

She made a pot of tea and had drunk an entire cup before Ella burst through the front door and came running into the kitchen.

'Sorry again, Bree. I got a bit side-tracked at Jenny's.'

Bree tutted. 'Discussing the strange woman, I suppose. Who is she anyway? All Lori told me was that her name was Cat, or something cat-related. Franklin couldn't recall. He said he wasn't really paying attention because he was hungry and wet and wanted to get home because they were going out for dinner.'

Ella sighed. 'It's Tabbie. Her name is Tabbie. Tabbie Talbaine. Did you make some tea?'

'Yes. Ten minutes ago. You'd better make a fresh pot.' Bree handed her the teapot and took her laptop out of her bag, placing it on the table in front of her. 'Have you Googled her?'

'Have I what?' Ella turned off the tap. 'I didn't hear you.'

'I asked if you'd Googled her.'

Ella looked surprised. 'No. I hadn't thought about that. That's the sort of thing Mia would tell me to do. God, I miss her. I can't wait for her to come home.'

'Same here.' Bree turned on her laptop and typed Tabbie's name into the search bar as soon as it appeared on the screen. A long list of results flashed up.

'Bloody hell, Ella. She's a bit of a celebrity.'

'She's what?' Ella spun round and dashed to Bree's side, looking over her shoulder at the huge number of images and articles popping up as Bree scrolled down.

'Tabbie Talbaine on the town,' Bree read out. '*Tabbie Talbaine's Tasty Titbits* – a blog by celebrity girl-about-town, Tabitha Talbaine.'

'Bloody Nora!' Ella said. 'That's the last thing I wanted to see. Not just beautiful, but famous too. And rich by the look of those designer clothes she's wearing in all the photos.'

Ella huffed out a sigh and marched over to the kettle, banging the teapot down on the counter so hard that Bree was surprised it didn't smash.

Bree tutted. 'So what? Gill's not going to be swept off his feet by fame and fortune. He's too level-headed for that. Oh. This one might cheer you up.'

Ella peered over Bree's shoulder.

'Or maybe not,' Bree added. Beneath the headline: *More of Tabbie's Tasty Titbits* was a photo of Tabbie standing on a luxury yacht, surrounded by tranquil, aquamarine waters with a red stone cliff in the background.

'So she also takes holidays on luxury yachts in exotic destinations. Thanks for pointing that out, Bree. Oh! Wait a minute. Go back to that photo.'

Bree had scrolled past it when she'd realised the photo definitely wouldn't make Ella feel better, and hoped that Ella hadn't noticed. But Ella pulled up a chair and sat beside her.

'Which one?' Bree asked, scrolling in the other direction, away from the photo.

'The other way. Go back up, Bree. Oh, give it to me.'

Ella snatched the laptop away and scrolled back up the screen, stopping suddenly, her mouth gaping open when she obviously found the photo.

'It must be awful to have people taking photos of you when that sort of thing happens,' Bree said, getting to her feet. 'I'll finish making the tea.'

Ella didn't say a word. She simply stared at the photo until Bree put the teapot on the table a few seconds later.

'Yeah,' Ella pushed the laptop back towards Bree. 'It must be a real pain to have such big boobs, but no bikini top that small was ever going to keep those massive jugs in place, was it? And did you notice that there weren't any tan lines?'

'Er, no. I didn't really study it.'

'Well, I did. And the woman obviously sunbathes topless most of the time. Her tan is even all over.'

'Um. She could've got it from a sunbed. Or it may even be a spray-on tan.'

'Nope. That suntan is real. And it's from being stretched out half naked on a no doubt tropical beach somewhere. Probably an island like the one Mia and Jet are on right now. Gill may not be swayed by fame or fortune but boobs like that are hard to ignore if they're thrust in your face. I wonder just how low cut that T-shirt was she was wearing today. I wish I could've seen her face-on but she had her back to me.'

'Oh come on, Ella. Now you're putting two and two together and making a farce out of it. Gill's not going to go all light-headed and stupid over a pair of boobs. No matter how large or perfect they may be, or how evenly tanned. He's just not that kind of guy. You know he's not.'

'Then why did he dash off and meet her, eh? Tell me that. And why didn't he even have the decency to tell me where he was going?'

The kitchen phone rang before Bree could answer Ella's question. Not that she had any idea what to say to reassure her.

Ella picked up the handset and a piece of paper floated to the floor. Ella bent down to pick it up and read the contents, glancing over at Bree, red-faced and smiling wanly.

'What?' she said down the phone. 'No. I don't need to type a special code into my laptop, because I don't have an undetectable virus that needs fixing. What? Oh for God's sake get a life, will you? Stop bothering people, you moron. If you really expect me to fall for a scam like that you're more delusional than I am. And the only problem I currently have with a laptop, is not one an idiot like you can fix.' She slammed the phone down, marched back to the table and threw the piece of paper at Bree. 'God, that man annoys me sometimes.'

'Er. The man who called? Does he do that often then?'

Ella scowled at her. 'What? No. I meant Gill. Gill annoys me. Read the damn note.'

Bree read out loud the words scribbled on the paper. '"Sorry sweetheart. Tabbie called and asked me if I could meet her in the pub because she wants to ask me some questions about Mattie and the village. As you and Bree are discussing her wedding, I didn't think you'd mind. I promise I won't be long. Say hi to Bree for me and I'll see you both soon. Gill." And there are three kisses. And a P.S. "Please don't eat my cake." And another kiss.'

'See what I mean?' Ella snapped. 'He is so bloody annoying.'

# Chapter Nine

Tabbie fiddled with the stem of her third glass of wine.

She hated this bit. She usually tried to keep it secret for as long as possible, but Gill was too nice to lie to, and he wasn't the type to take advantage of her. Not that spending an afternoon with the guy made her an expert on him and what he may or may not do, but she had a good feeling about him, and Tabbie had learnt to trust her feelings. Besides, she had been the one who had told him about her celebrity status.

'It's not really me who's the celebrity. It's my father.'

'Your father?'

She nodded but avoided meeting his eyes.

'Simon Saint Sorrel.'

'Um. I'm sorry, Tabbie, but I'm not really well-versed when it comes to celebrities. I've never heard of him.'

Now she did look at him. 'You've never heard of Simon Saint Sorrel?'

Gill shook his head. 'No. Sorry.'

She smiled wanly. 'I thought as you were into history, you would doubtless have heard of him. Perhaps it's too recent for you though. Thirty-three years is pretty modern, I suppose, all things considered.'

'I'm not sure I follow. Are you saying that your father was famous thirty-three years ago, or famous for something he did thirty-three years ago?'

'Both. He's still famous now. But perhaps only in certain circles. And strictly speaking, infamous is more apt.'

'Infamous?' Gill looked surprised.

Tabbie took a deep breath. 'Simon Saint Sorrel was the Chairman of Saint Sorrel's Bank, which had been around since the 1790s. Until my father embezzled several million and ran off with the nanny. The bank collapsed and it all caused quite a stir, to put it mildly. I was merely a baby at the time, so have no recollection of it of course, but some say he ran off with her and some say he murdered her and disposed of the body. Neither he nor my nanny has ever been found. Or the money. But like the Lochness Monster, sightings of him are reported from time to time. He seems to pop up all over the globe, but he's never popped up to visit me.'

'That must be difficult to deal with.' Gill reached out and squeezed her hand.

She gave him a grateful smile. 'I always think I've got used to it and then wham! Something happens and it all comes flooding back. My mother never speaks of him. Not even to say anything bad. Her life was hell for years after he left, but she bore it with grace and dignity and a steadfast determination to get through it. We had no money and we lived on the generosity of friends for a long time but she refused to drop his name from hers. She believed that would only make things worse. I, on the other hand, dropped it as soon as I could. Once I discovered the truth, that is. But I'll never be free of the connection.'

'Do you want to be?'

Tabbie sighed. 'I'm not entirely sure. I'd like to be free of the scandal. And although we knew nothing of his plans, my mother and I still feel the disgrace, somehow. I don't think we'll ever be free of that. Sometimes I imagine what it might be like to meet him. And I wonder if he's as bad as he's made out to be. But I try not to dwell on it too much. That way madness lies.'

'Forgive me for saying this, but have you considered writing a book about him? Don't look so surprised. You're a writer, after all.'

'I write blogs.'

'You're a writer no matter what you write. Blogs are like short stories. They're written to entertain. Writing a book about your father may not be light-hearted and fun, as you said you try to make your blog posts, but it might be cathartic. Writing definitely helps me deal with things I'd rather not. Face issues and subjects that are sometimes tough to handle. It's just a thought.'

Tabbie mulled over his words for a moment or two. 'And it's a good one. Even if I don't publish it, writing it all down might be just what I need to finally lay his ghost to rest, so to speak.'

'I'd be happy to help in any way I can, should you want me to.'

'That's very kind of you, Gill. I appreciate it more than you can imagine. But for now, what I'd really like you to help with is the research about Jennet de Witt and her descendants, all the way down the line to Aurelia. Some of the stories Aurelia told me last night and more this morning, were fascinating. There must be records from the 1600s. And maps, possibly. Aurelia mentioned the place where Jennet died, which is somewhere near Witt's Cottage but has been lost over time. It was known as The Witch's Tears, because of what happened there, but having told me about it, Aurelia then said she has no idea where it is. She says it was 'lost' many, many years ago. Possibly centuries. But I'm not sure I believe her. I think she may be lying to me about it, although I have no idea why. I believe it's some sort of rock formation, from something she said, but I may be wrong.'

Gill beamed at her. 'I'll be delighted to assist you. I could use a break from the book I'm working on. This will be fun in addition to being informative. It would be fantastic to know more about the village. There're more superstitions, myths and legends in this village than in any other place I've ever been or written about. Some actually appear to work, which is both amazing and troubling at one and the same time. Does this mean you'll be staying on for a while?'

Tabbie nodded. 'Aurelia has very kindly said that I may stay with her for as long as I please. I asked her if she would mind me doing some research into her ancestors and at first she seemed rather reluctant. She said that telling a friend about them was one thing but making their history public knowledge was a different matter entirely. I assured her I would tell her anything and everything I discovered and I wouldn't write anything in my blog that she was not completely happy about. Is that okay with you? It may be that after all our research, we can't write about any of it.'

Gill shrugged. 'Half the fun of it for me is simply doing the research. Discovering clues and snippets and stories and people long forgotten. I don't know Aurelia well. I've only lived in the village since last October, but I do respect her and her privacy, so yes. If she says we can't use any of it then we won't. Just knowing it is enough for me.'

Tabbie beamed at him. 'That's exactly how I feel. I knew I'd like you, Gill. I knew it the moment I saw you. When do you want to start? Is now a good time? Sorry, but as you'll soon discover, patience is not a virtue I possess.' She laughed cheerfully. She had not felt this good in a while.

'Oh Hell!' Having glanced at his watch, Gill leapt to his feet. 'We've been chatting for almost two hours. Ella will kill me. I've got to run, Tabbie. Um. May I give you a call later? I'll discuss it with Ella and work something out.'

'Of course. But do you need her permission? Sorry. That was rude of me.'

Gill laughed. 'No. I don't need her permission. But neither do I need her thinking I'm more interested in my computer and research than I am in her. The more she knows about what I'm working on, the happier we'll all be. Trust me on that. Bye for now.'

He waved to her and also to Alexia as he raced towards the door.

Tabbie shook her head as she watched him go. Ella was a very lucky woman.

# Chapter Ten

Ella sometimes forgot how lucky she was to have a man like Gill but most of the time she wondered how she got so lucky.

This wasn't one of those times.

'From now on,' she said, as he tore along the hall and kissed her on the cheek, 'whenever you leave me a note telling me you're 'just popping out' I'll realise that means you'll be gone for several hours without so much as a word.'

'You're annoyed? I suppose that's understandable. I'm sorry, Ella. I lost track of time.'

'That's not all you've lost.' She saw the look of concern spread across his face. 'You've lost your apple and cream turnover. Bree and I got tired of waiting for you, so we shared it.'

Relief swept over him. 'For a moment there I thought …' He coughed as he ran a hand through his hair. 'It doesn't matter. You and Bree were welcome to it.'

'Did you have fun?'

'I did.' Excitement filled his eyes. 'Tabbie wants me to help her with a project. We're going to be researching the history of this village and some of the families living here throughout the centuries. I'm rather excited.'

'I can tell.'

'Why are you giving me that look?'

'What look?'

'Something between suspicion and surprise.'

'Do I have anything to be suspicious or surprised about?'

'Of course not. That's why I asked what the look was for.'

'Hmm. This … project of the stunningly gorgeous Tabbie's – is there one particular century our latest celebrity visitor is interested in?'

Now Gill gave Ella a look something akin to suspicion and surprise.

'Has someone been gossiping about Tabbie already? Or did you Google her?'

'Does it matter? You haven't answered my question.'

He eyed her for a second before responding. 'Is something going on that I don't know about? You're acting a little oddly, even for you.'

'Even for me? What the hell does that mean? Are you saying I act odd? Oddly? Whatever. Are you saying I'm weird?'

He laughed nervously. 'You're the editor, sweetheart. And, yes. But in a good way. That's one of the things I love about you.'

'Oh really? What are the other things?'

'Sorry?'

'The other things you love about me, Gill. What are they?'

'Um. Far too many to mention. What's this all about, Ella? Is this because I wasn't here for tea with Bree? Or is there something else behind this attitude of yours?'

'Attitude of mine! You've got a nerve. I wasn't the one who disappeared for over an hour last night. Or who did the same today but for more than two hours. If anyone around here has an attitude problem it isn't me, Guillaume de Fonteneau!'

'Okay. Now I know you're mad. Not that kind of mad, before you shout at me. Mad as in angry. Furious, even. You only use my full name when you're really cross. What have I done to upset you?'

She glowered at him. 'The fact you need to ask merely proves to me that you're the one with the problem. I love you, Gill. Perhaps you need to decide if you still feel the same about me.'

'What? Of course I do. You really are mad if you doubt that.'

He laughed and tried to take her in his arms but she pushed him away.

'Your attempt at humour has failed. Perhaps you should go dashing off back to Tabbie Talbaine and her … tasty titbits.'

He let out a heavy sigh of irritation.

'That's what this is about? Tabbie? If you think I'm interested in her sexually, romantically, or in any way other than as a new friend and a research partner, you're mistaken. And deluded. I find the project far more enticing and exciting than the woman I'm helping. Next time we meet, I'll take you with me and then you can see for yourself.' He suddenly smiled. 'Are you jealous, Ella?'

'No I'm bloody well not. I'm just cross that you went to see her when you should've been here with me and Bree. That was rude of you and you're not usually a rude person.'

The smile faded. 'You're right. I'm sorry. I'll apologise to Bree. It was rude of me. It's simply that I get excited when I have a chance to talk to someone about history and the lives of people from previous eras. You know that. You know I love research. Uncovering clues and resolving mysteries is a passion of mine.'

'Yes. I do. I'd like to say it's one of the things I love about you. But at the moment, it's not. Oh. But as you're so excited about history and research, you should be overjoyed to know that Hettie wants you to dig something up for her. It's not a body or something in her garden before you ask. It's a map. A map of this village as it happens.

A map from the 1600s. It seems Tasty Tabbie isn't the only one who's doing research into this village in centuries gone by. While you're mulling that over, as I can see by your expression, you are, I'm popping out.' She walked towards the back door. 'And that means I'll be gone for at least an hour. Probably more.'

'What? Oh, very amusing.'

'Was it? My mistake. It wasn't meant to be.'

She slammed the door behind her as he called out her name. He wouldn't run after her. She knew that. He'd let her cool down and later, they might talk about it. Or not. They had had a couple of disagreements before. But this one was different.

Should she go back and apologise?

For what? For being cross. For being jealous. For being human.

Her feet sunk into the muddy sand on the dunes, the grass still wet and the sand damp from days of rain. The weather was miserable again. And so was she. Torrential rain was forecast. A storm was coming. Possibly in more ways than one.

She'd said things to Gill she hadn't meant to say. Hurtful things.

But so had he. That was so unlike him.

Something had undeniably changed in their relationship since Mia and Jet got married.

And it wasn't a change for the better.

It was definitely a change for the worse.

# Chapter Eleven

'Ella!'

Ella stopped. Had Gill chased after her? The voice on the wind didn't sound like his but perhaps the worsening weather had distorted it. She turned, smiling but her smile soon faded.

'Hello, Justin. And hello, Little M.' The dog was excited to see her and leapt up and down, splattering patches of wet sand from her paws all over Ella's jeans and jacket.

'Get down Little M,' Justin commanded but as he was laughing, Little M clearly thought it was a good game and jumped even higher, catching Ella on the nose with her claw.

'Ouch. Justin! Can you please put her back on her lead? I'm not in the mood to be mauled by a dog, however playful and loving she may be.'

'Sorry. Still trying to get to grips with this dog-sitting lark. Little M. Come here. Sit.'

This time his voice was firmer and he bit his lip to stop himself from laughing. Little M obeyed and Justin clipped on her collar, holding her a short distance away from Ella. The dog sat beside him, as good as gold, merely twisting her head and swivelling her neck when she spotted a gull, or a piece of dune-grass flying by.

'Thanks.'

Ella smiled at him and reached out and patted Little M's head which made the dog respond with a lick but as Ella had whipped her hand away, Little M licked thin air.

'No Gill?' Justin asked.

'We're not joined at the hip.'

'Oh dear. Do I detect a tear in the banner of blissful harmony?'

'Do what?' Ella burst out laughing. 'Who are you and what have you done with the real Justin Lake?'

Justin grinned. 'You might not believe me, but that's a line from the film I've just finished working on.'

'You're using lines from films now to talk to your friends?'

'And to chat up women.' He winked. 'Want to hear one?'

'Not particularly.'

'When I saw you, I understood the real meaning of beauty for the first time in my life.'

Ella raised her brows. 'When I heard those words, I understood the real meaning of nausea for the first time in my life.'

Justin sniggered. 'I've missed you, Ella. The people I hang out with in Hollywood simply don't get the importance of sarcasm.'

'Perhaps you're hanging out with the wrong people.'

'That's what I've been thinking. Rather a lot lately, as it happens. Are you heading somewhere?'

'In life generally, you mean, or right this second?'

'Both.'

'In life generally, apparently not. Right now, to Corner Cottage to get uncharacteristically drunk with Cathy and Christy.'

'How drunk is that? You used to get pretty out of it when we were dating.'

'What can I say? I'm a lush.'

He gave her a look of concern and reached out and touched her arm.

'Is everything okay, Ella? Seriously now. No joking.'

She held his gaze for a moment or two before nodding.

'Yeah. Everything's fine. Just the time of the month.'

'Oh God. I remember those.'

'From your own personal experience? Or do you mean you remember how my monthly cycle could sometimes affect me?'

'The latter.'

'Are you saying I was moody?'

'Why do I get the feeling that there's no right answer to that question? If I didn't know you better, I might think you were trying to start an argument.'

'You might be right. I told you. Time of the month.'

'Not sure I buy that, but hey. I'll go with it if it makes you happy. Can I walk with you to Corner Cottage? Sorry. May I walk with you? I don't want to get a detention for getting the old grammar wrong, do I?'

Ella grinned. 'You may. But don't expect a gold star. Or any jovial banter because I'm just not in the mood.'

'Cathy and Christy are sure as hell in for a good time then.'

'Better than you think. They don't know I'm coming. And I haven't even had the good manners to bring a bottle of wine. Good thing we're friends.'

They ambled along the sand for a few seconds, Ella kicking clumps of grass they passed and Little M trying to eat the clumps Ella had kicked.

Justin stopped abruptly and grabbed Ella's arm, turning her around to face him. Little M pulled on the lead to reach another clump of grass but sat, having clearly realised she couldn't make it.

'Okay. Are you going to tell me what's wrong? Or am I going to have to guess?'

'Nothing's wrong. I told you. Time of–'

'Bullshit. Don't give me that crap, Ella. We may not have dated for long but I think I know you better than that. Is it Gill? Are you having problems? Alexia told me when I popped into the pub just now that Gill was in there this afternoon with Tabbie. Are you jealous?'

'No.'

'Ella. Look at me. Are you jealous? Because I honestly don't think you have cause to be. I didn't really get to know Gill before I left last year – for obvious reasons. But since I've been back for the last couple of weeks, I've got to know him a bit more and there's one thing I can tell you for certain. The man is crazy about you. As crazy as Jet is about Mia. And we all know how crazy that is. Christ, my best friend who I'd known my entire life had a complete transformation in a matter of weeks after falling for her. Now that really is crazy. But nice, crazy.'

'Thanks. But to quote you earlier, "I'm not buying that." There is no way Gill feels even half as much for me as Jet feels for Mia.'

'Oh yeah? And you know that because …?'

'Because he … Because it doesn't matter how I know. I just know.'

'Oh. You can read minds now then, can you?'

'I don't have to. Actions speak louder than … No. That's not what I meant. But actions do speak louder and I can tell by his actions of late that he doesn't love me anywhere near as much as you say he does. And how would you know anyway? Jet may have had a complete transformation but you haven't. Have you ever been really in love, Justin?'

He shrugged. 'Once. A long time ago. But this isn't about me. It's about Gill and I know how much he loves you because he told me. He told all the guys, in fact.'

'When?'

'The night before the wedding when we were all together. He said that he knew how Jet felt because he had also found the love of his life and he never wanted to let her go because he wasn't sure he could live without her. That was you, in case you're wondering.'

'He said that? He really said that?' Wait. Was he drunk?'

'A little. But that just proves it. They say that when you're drunk you tell the truth.'

'Who says that?'

'Everyone. It's a fact. I think. Why do you always ask so many questions? The man loves you. He adores you. Accept it and deal with it and stop behaving like a moody little schoolgirl, okay? Hey. I've got an idea. You said Cathy and Christy didn't know you were coming, so why don't we give them a night of peace and quiet and you come home with me instead?'

'Justin! No. You've just been telling me how much my boyfriend loves me and now you're trying to get me to go to bed with you? That's disgusting.'

He looked surprised. 'I can recall when you couldn't wait to get into bed with me. And often, you didn't wait. You ripped my clothes off more than once in my bakery. But I wasn't trying to get you into bed. As I said, people tell the truth when they're drunk. Let's get you drunk and see what you have to say, shall we? I'll ask Bear and Alexia to join us so you know I won't try anything.'

'Why don't we just get drunk in the pub?'

'Because I've seen you drunk, and a public place is possibly not the best venue for that.'

'I don't want to tell the truth. I mean. There's nothing to tell. This is silly. This is ridiculous. I'm not going to Little Pond Farm with you. I'm not sure I even want to get drunk now.'

'Good. Then let's go to the pub instead and have a drink. And let's ask Gill and Tabbie to join us.'

'Gill and Tabbie? They're not a couple yet, you know.'

'And they never will be, Ella. Please stop being an idiot.'

'I'm not an idiot. But I'd rather not ask Gill and Tabbie to join us, if you don't mind. I'm not in the right mood to meet my competition.'

'I don't mind at all. I'm more than happy to spend a couple of hours in the pub with you. But she's not your competition, Ella. How many times do I have to say it? Gill is not going to ask her out.

I'd stake my life and my career on that. Besides, I rather fancy her myself.'

Ella sighed. 'Why doesn't that surprise me?'

Justin laughed, linked her arm through his, coaxed Little M to stand and headed back in the direction of The Frog and Lily.

'I'll tell you a secret, Ella. It surprised the hell out of me.'

# Chapter Twelve

'What on earth is wrong with Gill this morning, deary?' Hettie asked Ella, as Ella walked towards her.

Cathy, who was standing beside Hettie on the doorstep of Duckdown Cottage agreed.

'Yes. He was like a burglar who'd lost his bag of swag. Nearly jumped down my throat when I asked if you were in and whether it was okay for me to pop round and say hello.'

Ella grimaced. 'He's cross with me. I was coming to see Hettie. Is that okay?'

Hettie smiled. 'Of course it is, deary. You know you're always welcome here. I was going to watch darling little Daisy while Cathy visited you, but Fred can keep the sweetie-pie entertained while we three girls have a good old chinwag.'

'Where are Christy and Dylan?'

Cathy rolled her eyes. 'Dentist. And I don't know who had the biggest tantrum. Christy or little Dylan.'

She laughed as she stepped back inside Duckdown Cottage, Hettie standing aside to let both her and Ella in.

Hettie closed the door behind them. 'Go through to the sitting room, dears. I'll just pop to Fred's workshop and tell him to come and take over in the kitchen. The paints are out.'

She chuckled to herself as she walked towards the kitchen which led out to the garden and Fred's workshop-cum-shed-cum-mancave. She stroked Daisy's hair as she passed the kitchen table.

'Coo-ey, Fred, darling. I need you.'

Fred's head popped out of the half open door and a massive grin spread across his face, rippling his wrinkles and putting a sparkle into his elderly eyes.

'I thought we had company, my sexy little angel.'

Hettie gave a burst of laughter. 'Shush. You handsome devil. We do. And Ella's just popped in for a chat. Would you be a sweetheart and look after dear Daisy? I know you're trying to get the shelves I wanted, finished, but–'

'I'm hot on your heels,' he said, stepping out into the sunshine and closing the shed door behind him. 'If this lovely sun stays out, I'll take Daisy down to the beach for a paddle. May as well get out and make the most of it before it rains again.'

'What a good idea. Thank you, my darling.'

She kissed him on the lips and hand in hand they walked back into the kitchen.

'Want to nip down to the beach and see what's washed up on the shore?' Fred asked Daisy who was still sitting at the kitchen table, her tongue sticking out at one side of her mouth, her little brows furrowed in deep concentration.

Her head shot up and her eyes opened wide as she dropped her paintbrush, which rolled off the table and onto the kitchen floor splattering bright yellow paint across the tiles.

'Sorry, Grandma. Shall I clear it up?'

Hettie's heart nearly burst from her chest. 'No, my dearest darling. I rather like it, don't you? But maybe I'll clear it up later. You run along and have fun with Grandpa Fred. Don't forget to put your cardi on. It's warm in here and it's warming up nicely outside but there'll still be a chilly breeze down on the beach.'

'Yes Grandma.'

Daisy seemed to enjoy saying the word 'Grandma' almost as much as Hettie loved hearing it.

Daisy wasn't Hettie's real granddaughter, of course. Hettie had no children of her own. But since Leo, Hector's illegitimate son had started dating Cathy, who had, like Leo, come to the village for Christmas and never left, they had all begun to form an unlikely yet completely natural family bond. A bond that meant the world to Hettie. And to Fred too. A bond that only grew stronger day by day. A bond that both Cathy and Leo said they treasured. One that Hettie was determined would last for the rest of her days, no matter how long that might be.

Hettie loved Daisy as if the seven-year-old were her own flesh and blood, and Leo too, because he was Hector's flesh and blood. She loved Cathy because, well, because Leo loved her and that was good enough for Hettie. Add that to the fact that Cathy was a kind, caring and loving woman, who had been through her own trials and tribulations and that was enough for Hettie to welcome her with open arms.

Hettie watched Daisy take Fred's hand after Fred slipped Daisy's little red cardigan around the child's shoulders and told her to pop her arms inside. He grabbed her bright yellow raincoat from a hook near the door and tucked it under his arm. He had a way with children and it was clear that Daisy loved Fred too as she smiled up at him.

'Thank you, Grandpa.' She turned back and waved at Hettie as she stepped outside into the garden and the warm sunshine, which was growing stronger by the minute. 'See you later, Grandma.'

Hettie blew her a kiss. 'Oh yes, my dearest treasure. Grandma will see you later.'

She watched Daisy and Fred clamber over the sand dunes towards the sea and wiped away a tear before it had time to fall, took a deep breath, folded her arms beneath her ample chest and walked towards the sitting room.

'Anyone want to place a bet on which one of those two comes back soaking wet and covered in sand from head to foot, dears? I'll give you a hint. It won't be Daisy.'

She shook her head and chuckled as she sat in her plush new chair – the chair Fred had bought her just one week ago, to make sure she was comfortable.

'We can move it in front of the window if you like,' he'd said. 'Then you can watch everyone in Lily Pond Lane as they come and go.'

'Maybe later,' she'd replied. 'For now it's good where it is, right next to yours.'

They used to sit next to one another on the sofa, but that was old and it was getting so uncomfortable for Hettie now. Her new chair was so much better. It rose up at the press of a button and down again when another was pressed. It reclined and a footrest popped up. Even the back cushions plumped up on demand and the headrest could be adjusted to the perfect position.

'Ouch,' said Ella, slipping her hand beneath her bottom. 'Either there's a spring sticking out of this sofa, or you've dropped a pin or something. Or maybe Prince Gustav's got out and bitten me on the bum.'

'It's old, deary. But then aren't we all?'

'Oy. I'm not old.' Ella stood up and studied the seat. 'It's a spring. Look. Right there. Are you getting a new one?'

Hettie frowned. 'I hadn't realised it was quite that bad, dear. Perhaps.'

Cathy tutted but laughter filled her eyes and her voice. 'You are, Hettie Turner. Leo's already said that if you're not going to pick one yourself, he'll pick one for you and if you don't like it when it arrives, you've got no one but yourself to blame.'

'And as we told dear Leo, we can't have him buying us a sofa. We'll get around to it.'

'Nonsense.' Cathy glanced at Ella. 'Help me make them see sense, Ella. Leo can afford it and he's happy to do it. He wants to do it. And it'll benefit us too. We don't want to get a spring in our bottoms every time we come to visit. And what about Daisy, Hettie? Do you want her hurt by a nasty spring?'

'Of course not!' Hettie was shocked by that comment and sat bolt upright. 'I'd never want anything to hurt the dear little girl. Or you and Leo for that matter, dear. I hadn't thought about that. You're right. If Leo's sure he really doesn't mind, then we'll take him up on his kind offer to take us to the showroom. But he's not paying for it. We've still got money from the sale of Fred's house, which is how he bought me this wonderful chair. But he ordered this online from a specialist. We'd need to go to a store to try out sofas, dear, which is why we've put it off. Leo works so hard. We didn't want to spoil his weekend by traipsing around a furniture store until we needed to, that's all, dear.'

'Take my word for it, Hettie,' Ella said. 'You definitely need to.'

'That was easier than I thought,' Cathy said, beaming at Hettie and then at Ella. 'Phew. I'll phone Leo the minute I get back and tell him the good news. He'll be so pleased. But he'll still want to pay for it and I honestly think you should let him. He wants to do something nice for you and Fred, Hettie. Please let him do this.'

Hettie sighed. 'I can't see why buying us a sofa would make him so happy, but all right then. If he insists.'

'Yay.' Cathy waved her arms in the air, stopping suddenly, a horrified look on her face. 'Oh God, Ella. I was going to make some coffee. Honestly, I'm so forgetful these days. I don't know what's wrong with me. And tired too. Christy says it's the weather. The rain's been getting us all down. It's wonderful to see the sun at last.' She leant back in her seat and stared out of the window for a moment before bolting upright and jumping to her feet. 'There, you can see what I mean about my memory. I was going to make some coffee.'

She laughed as she hurried towards the kitchen.

Hettie glanced across at Ella. 'Why is Gill cross with you, deary?'

'What?'

Ella was fidgeting on the sofa, obviously trying to find a comfy spot and Hettie waited until she was settled.

'I asked why Gill is cross with you.'

'Oh right. Yes that. Um. Bit of a misunderstanding.'

'A row you mean, deary?'

Ella pulled a face. 'A difference of opinion. I'd rather not talk about it.'

Hettie crossed her arms beneath her chest. 'Well, if that's how you feel about it, I completely understand.'

'You do?'

'Yes, my dear. I do. We'll let the subject drop.'

'We will?'

Hettie nodded. 'So why were you coming to see me?'

'I wanted to ask you about the favour you were asking Gill. I assume that's why he was here this morning.'

'It was. Didn't he tell you he was coming? That's unlike the two of you.'

Ella shrugged. 'He was in bed last night and fast asleep when I got home. I didn't want to disturb him so I slept in one of the other bedrooms. He was gone this morning by the time I got up and I was going to ask if he'd been here. But you told me he had before I got to ask you.'

Hettie sighed. 'I know you said you don't want to talk about it dear, but clearly you do. Let's wait for Cathy to bring the coffee, shall we? She's far better at giving advice.'

Ella gave her the strangest look but neither said a word until Cathy returned a minute or two later with a tray bearing three mugs of coffee and a plate of chocolate digestives.

'I could murder one of those,' Ella said, grabbing a biscuit from the plate. 'You don't mind, do you?'

'Help yourself,' Hettie said, smiling at her. 'I had more than my share of biscuits when I worked for Mia last year and we sat around the kitchen table discussing Mattie and her will. To think, I hadn't even met Fred back then. So much has happened hasn't it, dears, and in such a short space of time?'

'Getting nostalgic, Hettie?' Ella asked, her mouth full of biscuit.

'A little, deary. So you were asking about Gill and my favour?'

'But why was he in such a strop?' Cathy queried. 'Have I missed that bit?'

'A misunderstanding,' Hettie said.

Cathy glanced at Ella. 'Oh, I see. You've had a row?'

Ella frowned. 'Not a row, exactly. There were no raised voices. Although I must admit, I suppose I did sort of storm out.'

'Sometimes that makes things worse. It's often better to get everything out in the open and try to resolve the issues. Never go to bed on an argument. That's what my granddad always told me.'

'They slept in separate beds last night,' Hettie confided.

'Thanks, Hettie.' Ella glared at her and grabbed another biscuit.

'Oh dear. That's never good.' Cathy shook her head. 'And this morning?'

'Gill was gone before she got up.'

Ella covered her mouth as she spat out biscuit crumbs.

'Hettie! I'll tell Cathy, thank you very much.'

Hettie shrugged and sipped her coffee.

'Gone?' Cathy tutted. 'You need to sort this out, Ella before it blows out of all proportion.'

'I will. When I know where Gill is. But for now I wanted to know about Hettie's favour.' She looked Hettie in the eye. 'You wanted him to find a map of the village, didn't you?'

Hettie shifted uncomfortably. 'Yes, deary. I did.'

'From the 1600s?'

Hettie nodded. 'Yes. Or around that time. Something from about 1612 up until about 1630 would be perfect. And any later maps too. Just in case.'

'In case of what? Why do you suddenly want an old map of the village?'

'I'm interested, that's all deary. All that intrigue with Mattie's will gave me a taste for it. I'd like to see what the village looked like back in the old days and see if everything is the same now as it was then. Taking into account that it's several centuries later.'

Ella stared at her. 'It's merely a coincidence then that this Tabbie woman arrives and wants Gill to help her research the history of the village from, oh guess what? The 1600s and onwards until the present day.'

Hettie's coffee went down the wrong path and she coughed and wheezed until Cathy took her mug from her and slapped her on the back.

'Are you okay, Hettie?' Cathy asked.

Hettie put a hand to her chest and nodded. 'Thank you dear. Yes, yes. I'm fine.'

'I didn't mean to upset you,' Ella said, perched on the edge of the sofa as if ready to fly to Hettie's aid; a contrite expression on her face.

Hettie smiled. 'You didn't upset me, dear. To answer your question, I have no idea why this Tabbie Talbaine wants to research the village history. I'd never heard of her until Gill told me about her today. He said it's because she's staying with …' Hettie found it hard to say the name out loud but she persevered. 'She's staying with … Aurelia Jenkins.'

'And?' Ella and Cathy asked in unison.

Hettie sighed. Ella was clearly not going to stop asking questions.

'Some people say Aurelia is descended from a long line of witches, dating back several centuries. Gill says Tabbie is interested in tracing the history back to Jennet de Witt, Aurelia's ancestor who came here in 1612.'

'Some people?' Ella furrowed her brows and leant forward. 'Not you, Hettie? You don't believe it? That's surprising, seeing as you were the one who told us all about every single myth, legend and weird superstition in this village. Including the curse of Frog's Hollow. You believe in all of those things but you don't believe in witches.'

'I didn't say I don't believe in witches!' Hettie banged her mug down on the coffee table.

'Wow! Okay, Hettie. No need to shout.'

'Calm yourself, Hettie.' Cathy placed a soothing arm around her.

Hettie shook her head and forced a smile. 'I didn't mean to snap, deary. I'm not sure if I truly believe that there are witches today, but I do believe that Jennet de Witt was a very powerful person in ways we don't understand. She escaped the Pendle Witch Trials and settled here. What I don't believe is that Aurelia inherited the gift.'

'Fair enough.' Ella smiled at her. 'That still doesn't explain why you want the map. And please don't give me that line about being interested in how the village looked centuries ago. Is it because there's a hidden treasure or something?'

Hettie sighed again. 'You and Gill are so alike. He wouldn't let it go either. Right you are, deary, I'll tell you why. But it mustn't go beyond this room. Yes. It's a hidden treasure. But not the sort of treasure you mean. It's not money, or trinkets or gold. It's water.'

'Water? We live beside the sea, Hettie. And there are three ponds in the village that I know of. One on the village green, Frog's Hollow and a small one on Jet's Farm. Oh, and Aurelia's pond, of course. The one Tabbie drove her car into. Why would you, or Tabbie if that's what she's doing, need to search for water? Wait. Don't tell me. If you walk through this particular bit of water it'll make you look like you're twenty again. But Tabbie doesn't look much older so she wouldn't need it for that.'

'Maybe it's water that gives you eternal life if you drink it,' Cathy suggested.

'Ah yes. The Holy Grail of waters. Naturally, it would be found in Little Pondale.'

Ella and Cathy both laughed but Hettie said, 'You may laugh about it, dears, but you're not far off the mark. This water is a natural spring. It's called The Witch's Tears after Jennet de Witt because she died there. I didn't tell Gill that part. I only told him I was looking for a natural spring that I'd heard my great grandmother talk about and that I wanted to see if Fred and I could find it. You know what Gill's like about superstitions and such, so I didn't want to mention it and besides, I don't recall the full story, but legend has it that if you drink The Witch's Tears and ask for the thing you most want, you'll get it.'

'Um. Doesn't The Wishing Tree do the same thing?'

'Not exactly, no. And that only works in December, deary. The Witch's Tears can be taken at any time.'

'You're serious, aren't you?' Ella said.

'Deadly serious, my dear.'

'But what could you possibly want?' Cathy asked.

'A new sofa for one thing,' Ella joked.

'Well, they're getting that so there's no need to find the weeping water or whatever it's called.'

Ella grinned. 'I like 'Weeping Water' more than 'The Witch's Tears'. It flows better. No pun intended.'

'You two youngsters may joke. But it's very powerful magic, so they say, my dears. So powerful that shortly after Jennet's death, one of her descendants hid it.'

'How do you hide water?' Cathy asked.

Ella shrugged. 'Search me. I don't mean that literally, of course. I don't have it. Although I do need to pee. May I use your loo?' She hurried towards the hall without waiting for a reply but stopped at the doorway. 'How did this Jennet witchy woman die?'

'She drowned.'

Ella spat out a laugh. 'Oh dear God. Now that really is funny. This powerful, magic water didn't do her much good, did it?'

# Chapter Thirteen

'You don't seem quite so jolly this morning.'

Tabbie had been watching Gill since the moment he arrived at Witt's Cottage and the cheerful man of yesterday had definitely been replaced by a grouch. Aurelia had cleared a table in the sitting room for them to work from and Gill had been banging his laptop, notepads and pencils around for the last fifteen minutes since they had sat down. He'd even spilt a cup of coffee all over one of his notebooks and he'd cursed, made a growling sound like an angry dog, and cursed again.

'Sorry. I had a bad night. I didn't get much sleep.' He slammed his laptop closed and turned to face her as she sat beside him. 'There's something I need to ask you.'

'Fire away.'

He took off his glasses and wiped the lens on the hem of his short sleeved, check, cotton shirt.

When he put them back in place, he still averted his eyes.

'You can ask me anything, Gill,' she coaxed. 'I told you about my father yesterday and I don't tell anyone about him, so believe me, I'll answer your question whatever it is.'

He glanced up at her. 'Why are you here? I mean, did you really come to Little Pondale to ask Aurelia to say something on video to your mother for her birthday? Or was that merely an excuse?'

'I'm not sure why you think I'd use my mother's birthday as an excuse to visit Aurelia. Or that there'd be some ulterior motive behind my visit. I hadn't planned to stay. I'm only here now because I accidentally drove my car into Aurelia's pond.'

'Was it an accident?'

'Of course it was, Gill!' Tabbie rose angrily from her seat and paced the room. 'You don't honestly think that I drove my beloved car into that ditch. I mean pond. I must remember it's a damn pond! You don't seriously think I did that on purpose?'

Gill shrugged. 'I find it hard to believe, but it's a very strange coincidence.'

'What is? What's this about, Gill?'

He met her eyes as she resumed her seat.

'It's about you and one of my neighbours both suddenly wanting to research what the village was like around the time of the 1600s. And both wanting a map. You asked me again if I could find a map the moment I arrived today.'

'Yes. Because I'd been thinking about our conversation in the pub yesterday, and one of the things I asked, was whether or not there may be some maps of the village from that time. Last night I had a dream about finding a map. So yes. It was the first thing I mentioned when you arrived. If I'd known that it would put you in such a foul mood, I wouldn't have asked, believe me. As for one of your neighbours asking for the same, or a similar thing, that's odd, I'll agree, but lots of people are interested in tracing their ancestors these days, so perhaps your neighbour wants to do that.'

'No. She wants to trace Aurelia's ancestors.'

Gill winced as if he hadn't meant to say that and a rose tinge crept into his cheeks. He removed his glasses and wiped them again.

'Well then, perhaps we should invite her to join us. I've got nothing to hide. No hidden agenda. No secrets to keep. I told you yesterday that I was fascinated by Aurelia's stories, and that they'd made me want to research the line back to Jennet de Witt. To find out who she was and what she did. How she lived and how she died. And what her ancestors did, all the way down to Aurelia. That's it.'

'So you've got no interest in finding a certain body of water?'

Tabbie laughed. 'Having spent longer than I'd have liked in a certain body of water the night before last, I can safely say a definite no to that. I'll make some more coffee. Unless you want to forget this and go home. It's fine with me if you do. I can do some research myself, so it's not a problem. Honestly. Please don't feel you have to stay if you'd rather not. Or if you think I'm hiding something from you and you can't trust me.'

They stared at one another for a moment or two until she waved her empty mug in the air.

'So what's it to be, Gill? Coffee? Or no coffee?'

'Aren't you going to ask me what the body of water is?'

'No. Because as I told you. I'm not interested in any water. Unless it's in the kettle and soon to be in my coffee mug.'

'And you're really only still here because of the accident?'

'For goodness sake, Gill. Yes. A genuine, if rather foolish, accident. Although I do think Aurelia should consider erecting a sign to warn people that what looks like a lane is actually her garden path. And what looks like a shallow, muddy ditch is actually a rather large, deep pond in the middle of what is not, as one might at first assume, overgrown hedgerows and fields but in fact, her garden.'

Gill grinned. 'I'm sorry, Tabbie. I'm a little crazy today. Coffee, please. If that's still okay with you?'

Tabbie smiled. 'It's better than okay. And I meant it, Gill. Your neighbour is welcome to join us, or to share in our research. I really have got nothing to hide. As I said, the only caveat I have is that if we find out something about one of Aurelia's ancestors, no matter how trivial or insignificant it might seem to us, we run it by Aurelia first. If she demands that we keep it to ourselves then that's what we do. Okay? This is her life and her history we're delving into and it may already be in the public domain for anyone to discover if they search long enough, but I'm not going to bring it to the fore if Aurelia would rather we didn't.'

'That's fine by me. As for my neighbour, she won't want to join us. I'll just get her the map she wants, if I can find one, and share anything with her that might help her find what she's looking for.'

'And I'm not going to ask what that is. I'm going to make that coffee.'

# Chapter Fourteen

'Hello, Ella.'

'Hello, Gill.' Ella swivelled around at the sound of his voice and was ready to run into his arms and tell him she was sorry for being so jealous, but the look in his eyes gave her pause. 'I'll make dinner now you're home. It'll be ready in half an hour. I would've started it sooner but I had no idea where you were or what time you'd be back.'

Why had she added that last bit? She hadn't meant to.

Gill sighed. 'Please don't start this again, Ella. I'm really not in the mood. And that goes both ways, you know. I had no idea where you were last night. Or even if you came home. Until I saw you in bed in one of the other rooms this morning. And you could've got in as the sun came up for all I know.'

'For your information, I was in the pub last night and I came home around midnight. You were fast asleep and rather than wake you, I slept in another room. You didn't bother to wake me this morning before you left to spend your day, no doubt, with Tabbie.'

'I did spend it with Tabbie. And we had a really good day, as it happens.'

'I bet you did. Well, I spent yesterday evening in the pub with Justin. And we had a really good time too.'

He glared at her. 'Good. Then we're both happy. I'm going to take a shower.'

'Fine.'

She watched him walk towards the stairs and frustration twisted and turned inside her. She clenched her fists and grit her teeth as she filled a saucepan with water and banged it down on the hob.

She opened a bottle of wine and poured herself a glass, knocking back the contents in several large gulps. That would make her feel better. That would calm her down and settle her thoughts.

But it didn't. So she poured herself another.

If only he'd come in and smiled at her instead of having such a guarded expression on his face – as if he had something to hide. Or felt guilty or something.

She opened a jar of olives and popped two in her mouth.

Was that it? Did he feel guilty?

He did say he and that Tabbie woman had a really good day. What did that mean? And just how good had it been?

Good enough that he needed a shower before he gave Ella a kiss, as he usually did when they hadn't seen one another for several hours. A long, slow, sensual kiss. The sort of kiss that reminded her he loved her.

Not that she had needed reminding of that until recently.

Ever since the wedding.

Perhaps he'd been giving someone else long, slow, sensual kisses all day.

Her blood boiled faster than the water in the pan she'd put on the stove to cook the pasta.

She marched along the hall and stood at the foot of the stairs.

'Gill?' she shouted up as she heard the shower turn on. Until recently, she'd have raced up those stairs and jumped in the shower with him.

Tabbie's face flashed before her, together with those large, perfect breasts.

Suddenly Ella was imagining Tabbie in the shower with Gill, and Gill's hands were all over her. Caressing, teasing, tantalising.

Ella fumed. The bastard!

But wait. Wasn't this ridiculous?

Was Gill really the type of guy who would cheat on his girlfriend and still come home and have dinner with her?

But if he wasn't cheating on her, why hadn't he kissed her when he came in?

'Gill,' she shouted up the stairs again. 'I'm going for a walk.' And when he didn't reply she yelled. 'You can make your own bloody dinner.'

# Chapter Fifteen

'Hi Glen.'

Ella stood at the front door of Rectory Cottage, her blonde curls plastered flat against her head by the sudden but not totally unexpected downpour.

Glen quickly stepped aside to let her in.

'Come in, come in. You're saturated. Let me take your jacket. Don't you have an umbrella?'

Ella hurried into the hall and removed her sodden, lightweight, supposedly waterproof jacket and handed the dripping item to the vicar.

'Not with me, no. It wasn't raining when I came out, and I was only going for a quick walk to clear my head. But it didn't work, so that's why I'm here. I hope you don't mind, but I could really do with some advice.'

'I don't mind at all. Let's go through to the kitchen and I'll make some tea.'

He led the way along the hall, holding Ella's jacket as far away from himself as he could, leaving a trail of water the length of the hall and beyond.

'Sorry about my jacket,' Ella said, following behind him.

'It's only water.' Glen smiled at her as he placed the garment across the back of a chair which he moved closer to the Aga. He nodded to the remaining chairs around the kitchen table. 'Please take a pew. I'll put the kettle on. What sort of advice are you after? Spiritual or general?'

'Spiritual?' Ella's cocked an eyebrow and a droplet of rainwater ran down her cheek. She wiped it away with the back of her hand. 'Please, Glen. It's me.'

He grinned and tossed her a hand towel he took from a drawer in the dresser.

'Ah yes. A non-believer. Silly me. How can I help?'

She rubbed her face, arms, hands and finally her hair as dry as possible and passed the damp towel back to him. He walked to the small utility room attached to the kitchen and tossed the towel in a basket.

'I'm not sure you can. But with Mia away, I didn't know who else to turn to.'

'I'm glad you felt able to come to me.' He flushed slightly. 'I'm not an expert on women's issues but I'll help as much as I possibly can.' He leant against the worktop and smiled reassuringly.

'Women's issues? Oh God, Glen. I'm not here to ask your advice about my periods or anything.'

She gave a burst of laughter. 'I'm here to get a man's point of view. Garrick's been no help at all. He told me the other day that I'm being my 'usual self' whatever that means, and that it's time I grew up and behaved like a responsible adult. But Gill's behaving the same. He didn't say Gill should grow up. Franklin's American, so I'm not sure he understands the psyche of an English male. And Justin was even less help. All he did was get me drunk, which of course made things worse because I didn't get home till after midnight and slept in another bed and that made him even more cross than he was before. Fred's too old to understand and Bear's not the best person to ask. Great for a medical issue but not so hot where romance is concerned. Although he did eventually get the woman he'd always wanted, so perhaps he's not so bad, after all. Jet's the one I would've asked as well as Mia, but he's not here, of course. And Toby and I have never really been close. That's probably because of everything that happened with Alexia. Anyway. That's why I came to you.'

'Hmm. I'm not sure I followed all of that and I may need some clarification on parts, but what I believe you're saying is you've got a romance-related problem and, having discussed it with everyone possible, I'm your last resort. And I'm assuming, as you said Gill's behaving the same, and you've only asked males, it's concerning Gill.'

Ella nodded. 'But I haven't only asked males. I've asked Cathy, Hettie, Jenny and Lori. They all said I should talk to him and sort things out. But how can I talk to him? I tried tonight but he didn't even kiss me hello and he was in such a hurry to take a shower that I naturally reasoned he might've been having sex with her. He did say they'd had a really good time. But if I ask if he's going off me, and if he fancies Tabbie more, he's hardly likely to admit it, is he? And he's not going to admit to the sex bit. Not unless he wants to sleep on the street tonight. Although I suppose Tabbie would welcome him with open arms. And open everything else too.'

'Tabbie? The woman staying with Aurelia? Are you saying you think Gill may be having an affair with her? Seriously, Ella?'

Ella nodded. 'That's exactly what I'm saying.'

The kettle boiled and Glen turned to make the tea.

'I find that very hard to believe. But let's start at the beginning shall we and see where we go from there?'

# Chapter Sixteen

'Thanks again for last night, Jenny,' Ella said, leaning an arm on the top of the glass, display cabinet in Lake's Bakes the following day. 'My talk with Glen helped but having dinner with the two of you and chilling out and watching a movie afterwards, helped even more. Although it did mean that when I got home, Gill was already in bed, so we still didn't talk. But I did what you and Glen said I should, and slept in our bed, not one of the other rooms.'

'It was our pleasure. You know we're always here for you. Did you and Gill talk this morning?'

Ella sighed. 'Nope. I overslept. Again. But there was a mug of coffee beside the bed when I woke up. Cold coffee. It had obviously been there for some time, but at least it's a step in the right direction. He didn't simply get up and walk out. He stopped to make me coffee. He may've tried to wake me up, but as Mia will tell you, I could sleep through Armageddon.'

'Really? I loved that film. I know he's a bit old for me, but I've always had a thing for Bruce Willis. I think it's that sexy smile of his and there's definitely a twinkle in his eyes.'

'What? Not the film, you twit.' Ella grinned at her. 'The biblical event. The battle to end all battles. Good and evil fighting it out before the end of the world. The final conflict before the Day of Judgement. Er. For someone who's dating a vicar, you're not very up on your New Testament, are you? I know what Armageddon is and I'm not even religious.'

Jenny giggled. 'You can be such a smart-arse sometimes. I've heard of Armageddon. It simply didn't click. I didn't get much sleep last night. We didn't get to bed until gone midnight and then Glen was in a very romantic mood.'

'Is that a somewhat twee way of saying you had all-night sex? Which is also a twee way of saying that you F–'

'Yes, Ella. Thank you. We don't use the F-word in my bakery.' Jenny winked. 'But we did. Like rabbits.'

'Lucky you. The last time Gill and I had … were *romantic* was nearly a week ago. Shit!'

'Ella! We don't use the s-word either.'

'Sorry. But I hadn't realised it was so long.' She slumped her other arm on the glass top and sighed. 'Oh God, Jenny. What am I going to do?'

'Talk to him, Ella. You can't go on like this. It's ridiculous. When Mia and Jet had their misunderstanding they didn't let it come between them. They talked about it.'

'Yeah. But they were both willing to. They both wanted to. I'm not sure Gill wants to talk about it. Last night he made it clear he didn't.'

'No. From what you told us, he made it clear he didn't want to bicker about it. Talking and bickering are completely different. Bickering is about tossing accusations around, finding fault and blaming one another. Talking is about listening and sharing and being willing to meet the other person halfway.'

'Now who's being a smart-arse. Okay, okay. I'll talk to him. If I ever get a chance. God, I'm dying for a coffee. You know what you need, Jenny?'

'A good night's sleep.'

'Apart from that. You need a little café in here.'

Jenny gave Ella a look of surprise.

'You must be able to read my mind. Only the other day, as I stood here in an empty shop, watching yet another torrential downpour, I wished I had a café attached to the bakery. Then people wouldn't simply pop in and out for bread and cakes, they'd stop and chat.'

'Doesn't everyone who comes in here stop and chat already? I was thinking more along the lines of people being able to get a cup of coffee while they were chatting.'

'That's what I meant too.'

'And it would make you extra dosh.'

'That's true. But there simply isn't room. It'll just have to be my secret wish.'

'It's not a secret because I know about it. And there is room. At least for one table and a couple of chairs. One of those bistro tables would fit in that corner. And in the summer, you could have table and chairs outside. Or across the lane on the village green.'

'I'd probably need planning permission or something for that, but you're right about a bistro table. One would fit in that corner. Why didn't I think of that?'

'Because you're not as brilliant as me.' Ella laughed and winked at Jenny.

'Oh yeah? Well, I may not be as brilliant, but at least I'm having sex. Sorry. That wasn't funny. I didn't mean it.'

'Don't worry about it. Listen. There's an old bistro-type table on the garden deck of Sunbeam Cottage. We've got lots of other tables and seating out there, so we could make do without that one for now. It'll give you an idea of what it looks like and whether it would work.'

'That sounds perfect. Thanks, Ella. That's a fantastic idea.'

'I'll get Garrick to pop it over later today. He says he's actually going to spend tonight at our place. Since he and Bree got engaged he's been as good as living at Willow Cottage with her. Which really doesn't make sense because Sunbeam

Cottage is at least twice the size, if not more, of Bree's place.'

'But Willow Cottage gives them privacy and a certain amount of peace and quiet.'

'You're saying Gill and I are noisy? Okay. Maybe I am. But I'm not as noisy as Flora can be. When that kid cries, people in China know about it. And when the twins are born, Sunbeam Cottage will seem like a sanctuary. Even with me in it.'

'Has Garrick said where they're going to live once the twins are here? I suppose, as Willow Cottage has two bedrooms and Flora will still only be just over one year old, all three babies could fit in the second bedroom. But it's clearly not a long-term option.'

Ella frowned. 'I hadn't even considered that. Really, when you think about it logically, Garrick and Bree and the three kids should move into Sunbeam Cottage and Gill and I – assuming there is still a 'Gill and I' by then, should move into Willow Cottage. But as both properties belong to Mia and Jet, I suppose it's up to them who lives where, not us. God. I hope we can work something out. Is it just me, Jenny, or does it feel like, ever since the wedding, everything's changing? And not necessarily for the better.'

# Chapter Seventeen

So Ella wasn't the only one who thought things had changed since the wedding. Jenny had said that she and Glen had also noticed one or two subtle differences in certain people's behaviour.

Bree was obviously having mood swings caused by pregnancy so she didn't really count, and Garrick was understandably nervous. Having already lost one partner, he was naturally a little anxious. Everyone in the village knew that Bree's pregnancy was nothing short of a miracle. They were all wishing and praying that the birth would go like a dream. But as the twins weren't due until next February, it was a long time for those little anxieties to simmer away in the background.

Hettie had definitely been acting weird. This map business and wanting to find the natural spring of legend was an unusual and slightly bizarre quest for her. Ella still couldn't figure out why Hettie wanted so badly to find it. What she could possibly be wishing for at her age? Other than a longer life, perhaps.

Oh no! Was that it? Did Hettie think she was going to die soon? Not such an irrational thought as Hettie was in her eighties, but one Ella couldn't bring herself to consider. Why wouldn't the annoying woman simply tell them why she wanted to find it? She was quick enough to share everyone else's secrets with anyone who would listen. It was completely unreasonable of her not to agree to share her own. All she'd said was that drinking the water meant she could get the thing she most wanted, but flatly refused to say exactly what that was.

And Fred was no help. When Ella had taken him to one side after he returned from the beach with Daisy and asked if he knew why Hettie was so eager to find it, all he said was, 'I think you should ask Hettie that, dear.'

Ella's mood darkened as she squelched across the village green, back towards Sunbeam Cottage. The heavy grey clouds rolling in from the sea and threatening more rain, didn't do anything to improve it. As if they hadn't had enough already. If this weird weather continued, Hettie would never find her hidden spring of tears. The entire village would be under water. Ella shook her head. Perhaps she should ask Garrick to forget making his intricately carved and designed wooden furniture and build an ark instead.

She was so engrossed with her melancholy thoughts, she didn't spot the figure walking towards her and jumped when she heard her name.

'Ella? Excuse me, but are you Ella Swann?'

Ella glanced round. She recognised Tabbie Talbaine from the photos she and Bree had seen of the woman in their Google search. Immediately, she straightened her spine and pushed back her shoulders. If she'd had a sword to hand, she would've removed it from its sheath in readiness for battle.

'Yes. I'm Ella Swann.'

She was more than a little surprised when Tabbie smiled and held out her hand in a warm and friendly greeting.

'Oh, Ella, hello. I've been longing to meet you. I'm Tabbie. Tabbie Talbaine. I'm the one who's been taking up so much of your boyfriend's time, for which I must apologise. But he's a godsend. He really is. As if I need to tell you that. We've already uncovered far more than I had hoped we would. And it's fascinating. Truly exciting. But he's no doubt told you all about it. Anyway, I spotted you and from the things Gill's told me, I was sure you must be Ella. I was on my way to get some cakes from Lake's Bakes because Gill says that they're to die for. Aurelia makes delicious cakes, but Gill says you haven't tasted heaven until you've had one of Jenny's cream buns.'

'Gill's been saying quite a lot by the sounds of it. But he's right about Jenny's cakes. Er. Perhaps you'd be good enough to tell my boyfriend that, if he can find the time to drag himself away from his dusty old books and keep his laptop, and everything else, closed for a while, he could come home and see his girlfriend. She has something very important she'd rather like to talk to him about.'

'I'm sorry. Have I said or done something to upset you? You seem a trifle displeased. It's because I've been monopolising him, isn't it? I understand completely. But we both get so caught up in it that the hours simply fly. One minute it's nine in the morning, the next, it's six in the evening and we have no idea where the day has gone. I'll be sure to give him your message if I see him before you, which I doubt, and I promise I'll keep a closer eye on the time from now on. Although you're very welcome to join us if you'd like to.'

'Thank you, but no. I have my own work to do. I'm an editor, you know. Wait. You just said you'll give him my message if you see him before I do. What did you mean by that?'

'Gill told me you're an editor. An excellent one. And I didn't mean anything, other than in all probability you'll see him before I do today.'

Ella frowned. 'You're buying him a cream bun. You'll obviously see him before me.'

'Um. I'm not. I'm buying Aurelia and myself, cream buns. On Gill's recommendation. He told me yesterday that he'd be working from home today and nipping over to Little Whitting… something or other. I can't recall the name. He said he'd pop in later, but only for half an hour or so.'

Ella shot a look towards Sunbeam Cottage. The car was in the drive. It hadn't been there when she'd left to go to Lake's Bakes less than twenty minutes ago.

'He's working from home.' Ella smiled at Tabbie. 'Great. Thanks. Enjoy your cakes. See you later.'

'It was lovely to meet you,' Tabbie said, as Ella hurried away.

'Yeah. Same here. Whatever.'

Ella dashed up the drive and raced into the hall.

'Gill? Gill, are you here? Gill?'

He rushed into the hall from the dining room.

'I'm here. What's happened? What's wrong?'

There was a worried look on his face and Ella smiled as she breathed a sigh of relief.

'Nothing. I saw the car and wondered where you were.'

He let out sigh far louder than hers.

'Then why did you scream my name at the top of your lungs? Jesus, Ella. You nearly gave me a heart attack. I thought something terrible had happened.'

'It nearly did. It still might. But I'm wishing with all my heart that it won't.'

'What? I don't understand. Are you trying to tell me something?'

'Yes, Gill. I am. I think we need to talk.'

Colour drained from his face and he removed his glasses.

'This isn't a good time, Ella. Can't it wait?'

'It can, I suppose. But I don't think it should. Can't you leave whatever it is you're doing for now? This won't take long. At least I hope it won't.'

He sucked in a breath and slid his glasses back in place.

'You're going to tell me that's it's over, aren't you?'

'What? No. That's what I was hoping you'd tell me.'

'I beg your pardon? You want *me* to be the one to end this? Seriously?'

'Oh. I … I thought you had ended it. When Tabbie said just now that you're working at home today, I thought that meant it was over.'

He looked utterly confused. 'What has Tabbie got to do with it? Or where I'm working?'

Ella frowned at him. 'She's got everything to do with it. I thought your crush on her was the nail in the coffin of our relationship. But if you're over that, perhaps it isn't. Perhaps we can still sort things out.'

'Over what? I don't have a crush on Tabbie. What are you talking about, Ella?'

'You've been spending every second with her since the moment she arrived. I know things were a little odd between us before that but it got far worse when she appeared on the scene. I do need to know though. Has anything actually happened between you?'

'Between me and Tabbie? Are you serious, Ella? The only reason I wanted to spend time with Tabbie, was because burying myself in research for her project helped to stop me thinking about you and Justin.'

Ella's mouth dropped open.

'Me and Justin?' she eventually managed. 'There is no me and Justin. We're merely friends.'

'And former lovers.'

'Yes. But note the word, "former". That means precisely what it says. Besides, that's a pretty lame excuse. You couldn't care less about me and Justin. You didn't bat even as much as one little eyelash when he asked me to dance at the wedding. 'You actually said, "Be my guest", so don't use him as an excuse for your little fling with cat woman.'

'I didn't have a fling with cat – I mean, with Tabbie. Little or otherwise. And what did you want me to say? Don't come anywhere near my girlfriend or I'll deck you?' He sucked in a breath. 'Did you just nod? Bloody hell, Ella. Is that what you want? Men fighting over you. Justin and I are friends. Although I'm not happy about what's been going on. Not happy at all.'

'I didn't say that, but it wouldn't be the worst thing that could've happened. The worst thing is my boyfriend acting like he didn't give a damn.'

'Didn't give a damn? I was eaten up with jealousy! Watching the two of you, arms wrapped around one another, staring into each other's eyes and laughing like there was no one else in the world. Christ. I nearly did come over and punch him. I wanted to march over and drag you away. But I'm not a Neanderthal. And I told myself I was being stupid. That you loved me and that you and he were, as you say, just friends. Which would be fine, even though I'd still feel jealous. But–'

'Really? You really wanted to do that? To drag me off somewhere? Like to a cave or something? And then ravish me? I wouldn't have minded that one bit. Next time, bear that in mind, will you?'

'Next time? Is there going to be a next time?'

'Well, unless you're saying I can't ever dance with any man other than you, yes. There's going to be a next time. But don't actually hit anyone because that would be bad. And don't drag me off either because only bullies drag people around. Just ask me nicely. Simply say, "Ella, will you please come with me so that I can make mad, passionate love to you?" Okay?'

'And you'd come with me, would you? Even now?'

'Of course I would. Don't you know that?'

'The events of the last couple of days seem to indicate otherwise.'

'Because I lost my temper over you and Tabbie?'

'Once again, Ella, there is no me and Tabbie. I was referring to you and Justin.'

'And once again, Gill, there is no me and Justin. Nothing happened between us the other night. We merely talked. About you, as it happens. And last night I spent the entire evening discussing the same thing with Jenny and Glen. About how worried I am that I might lose you.'

'Lose me? Why would you think you'd lose me?'

'Because since the wedding things have been a bit odd between us. It was as if you were backing away. And I was scared. I love you, Gill. In fact, I adore you. I'd go anywhere with you. Even though sometimes you're bloody annoying.'

A smile spread slowly across his face and he took a step towards her.

'You mean that?'

'Of course I do.'

'I feel the same about you, Ella.'

'You do? Really?'

'I do.' He grinned. 'And you'd go anywhere with me? Even to Margate?'

She hesitated and a small furrow creased her brow. 'Yes. Especially to Margate.'

He took another step towards her before hesitating. 'Wait there. Don't move an inch. I mean it, Ella. Not an inch.'

He raced upstairs but was only gone for a minute or two before he came thundering back down, taking two stairs at a time.

'I haven't moved an inch. I haven't even moved a muscle.'

'Excellent. It's good to see that you're learning how to obey me. That'll come in useful for the future.' He winked at her and smiled.

'Obey you? Hmm. Good luck with that.'

She smiled back, her heart fluttering like a caged bird longing to break free and – in this case, throw her arms around Gill and smother him in passionate kisses, but she didn't move.

Gill coughed, removed his glasses, checked the lens and put them back on without wiping them. Then he took a deep breath and in a voice crackling with nervous energy said, 'I'm nowhere near as wealthy as Justin will be, but with the inheritance from my grandfather's estate, and the money from my books, I think I can afford somewhere a bit more exotic than Margate for our honeymoon.'

'For our … Did you say honeymoon? Are you … are you asking me to marry you?' She blinked several times as she stared into his eyes.

'Yes, Ella Swann. I'm asking you to marry me.' He got down on one knee and produced a ring, as if by magic, from the front pocket of his jeans.

'How long have you had that? Is that why you just dashed upstairs? I thought you were merely desperate for a pee.'

'No, Ella. I went to get the ring. I've had it since the week before Tabbie drove her car into Aurelia's pond.'

'The week before? But wait. That would've been about one week after Mia and Jet left for their honeymoon.'

Gill nodded.

'Then why didn't you ask me? Why did you act so weird every time I mentioned Mia and Jet's wedding? Or their honeymoon? Or Bree and Garrick's wedding?'

He shook his head and took another deep breath.

'Because it suddenly occurred to me that you might think the only reason I was proposing was because everyone else was getting married. Or worse still, that I was only proposing because I was worried you might run off with Justin. Which of course I was. And that got me thinking even more. You're always saying that I'm posh. I know it's a joke, but I started feeling that perhaps, in some way, you were making fun of me. That I didn't match up to the hunk that is Justin Lake. Or that I wasn't as good in bed as Justin. Or as passionate. Or as virile. I know I'm not as good-looking as him. Or anything at all in any way like him, come to that.'

'But I don't want Justin. I want you.'

'Well, I wasn't sure you did. Not forever, at least. I started wondering if you only dated me last year because you knew Justin was leaving. Or whether you started dating me hoping to make him jealous and that after he left, you simply continued dating me because there was no Justin around anymore.'

'I ended it with Justin because I fell in love with you, you jerk. Sorry. You're not a jerk. You're a wonderful, kind, caring and passionate man. And I love you.'

He smiled at her. 'Finally, I didn't ask you because I started worrying that you might say no. At least if I didn't ask you, you couldn't do that.'

'That's just silly.'

'I wasn't thinking clearly. Love makes us do crazy things. Feel crazy things. I mean look at the way we've both been behaving this week. We've both been more than a little crazy.'

She nodded. 'Ain't that the truth?'

'And I'm still waiting for an answer, Ella.'

'An answer? To what? Oh God! Yes! Yes of course I'll marry you, you idiot.'

He raised his brows. 'Not quite the romantic acceptance I'd hoped for but I'll take it.'

She ran to him, yanked him to his feet, and threw herself into his arms, wrapping her legs around his waist as she kissed him.

'Better?'

He smiled. 'Much. You definitely want to marry me? To spend the rest of your life with me? Because that's what this means, Ella.'

'Try and stop me. I'll drag you down the aisle if I have to.'

He laughed. 'Bully. So, shall I book one week in Margate, or really splash out and make it two?'

'Why go all the way to Margate when there's a perfectly good beach right here? And a pub that serves great food and a shop nearby that sells the most delicious cheese. I happen to know of a cosy little thatched cottage that I'm sure we can get. It's called Sunbeam Cottage and I think we can have it for more than two weeks.'

'Sounds like heaven.'

'It is, Gill. Pure, unadulterated heaven. And it will be. For ever and ever.'

He gave another little cough before smiling into her eyes as he slipped the ring on her finger.

'Ella, will you please come with me so that I can make mad, passionate love to you?' His smile grew wider. 'Did I get that right?'

'Word perfect, Gill. But then you are, aren't you? Perfect, I mean. Absolutely, bloody perfect.'

# Chapter Eighteen

Tabbie stopped on the village green, a short distance away from Lake's Bakes and watched as the stunning girl with the wild red hair, stood with her back to Justin, who was twirling her tresses into what appeared to be a casual bun. Both of them were laughing and judging by the playful slaps they were giving one another it was clear that these two were more than just friends. They were close. Very close.

A wave of disappointment swept over her and for a moment she hesitated. Part of her wanted to turn and walk away. But she had told Aurelia she was going out to get some cakes and it would be both rude and unreasonable to return empty handed.

Since the evening of her accident, Tabbie had been hoping to bump into Justin again. She had hoped he might call round to see what had happened regarding her car. But he hadn't.

She had planned to go to Little Pond Farm, which was where Aurelia had told her he was staying – looking after Jet and Mia's dog, apparently, but as yet, she hadn't made it. She had asked Aurelia where he lived and for how long he would be in Little Pondale. All Aurelia had said was that she wasn't sure where Justin called home right now and had no idea how long he'd be staying.

'You'll need to ask him if you want to know the answers to those questions,' Aurelia had said.

Which seemed a little odd, even for Aurelia. But then in the few days Tabbie had known her, there was one thing she had learnt. Aurelia was a little odd. Perhaps more than just a little.

Tabbie had spent so much time with Aurelia, listening to her fascinating tales, and then even more time with Gill, researching Aurelia's line, that she had hardly been away from Witt's Cottage. She had only been to The Frog and Lily once, which was the day she met Gill there to ask for his help. She'd met hardly anyone from the village, apart from the three 'boys' and Alexia, the barmaid at the pub. She'd been so happy when she spotted Ella.

But that meeting hadn't gone quite as she had hoped, although Ella seemed a little more friendly by the time she had rushed off into Sunbeam Cottage, so perhaps there was hope for a future friendship.

Not that Tabbie planned to be around for that much longer. She'd finally heard back from her insurers and they'd agreed to a courtesy car. But Justin had been correct when he'd said he thought her car would probably be a write-off. It wasn't only her bonnet that had been dented when she'd driven into Aurelia's pond. There must have been some rocks hidden in those murky waters because the length of her exhaust pipe had cracks in several places, both front axles had been broken, together with the radiator and the steering shaft, plus lots of other moving – or now not moving – parts would need replacing. Added to that the cost of drying it out and having it professionally cleaned, and the insurers had decided it wasn't worth the cost.

She didn't relish the prospect of finding another car, but she could think about that later. For now all she could think about was that she wished she could be in that redhead's shoes. Justin had swept the woman up in his arms and was twisting her around the small empty space in the corner of the bakery. The woman must be Jenny. And from the look of it, Justin was interested in more than Jenny's cream buns.

Tabbie stepped carefully between several puddles. If there was more rain and these pools of water joined up, it would be difficult to see where the village pond began or ended. All the ground around was saturated. Thank goodness Aurelia had lent her some wellies.

She glanced up at the sign swinging outside the bakery as she got nearer. Where had the name, Lake's Bakes come from? The village green looked a little like a lake right now, but surely it couldn't be because of that? Aurelia had said she hadn't seen rain like this for many years, and that sign was clearly fairly new.

Lake's Bakes had a jolly sound. Perhaps the baker's surname was Lake. Perhaps–

Tabbie stopped in her tracks.

Justin Lake, the Hollywood star had been a baker in a small village somewhere on the south coast. Tabbie had read that in a magazine.

It couldn't be. Surely all the villagers would be crowding around, making a fuss of him and telling all and sundry that he was here.

And yet. She had seen the likeness immediately the night they met. His name was Justin. He was staying at his friend's farmhouse. And she was standing outside a bakery called Lake's Bakes. That many coincidences added up to one big fact. Justin was Justin Lake, Hollywood heartthrob, tipped to be a superstar. The man had the world at his feet. And women too.

Was he waving?

Yes, he was. He had put Jenny down and he was waving.

Tabbie swivelled to her left and then her right but there was no one else in sight.

He was waving at her.

Her knees wobbled, her legs had turned to rock and her wellies were held in a firm grip by the mud, or so it seemed.

He pushed open the door and beamed at her.

'You'll get soaked,' he shouted.

She hadn't even noticed it had started raining again.

'Quick,' Jenny yelled. 'Come in out of this weather.'

She managed to free her wellies and she dashed towards the door, tripping over the step and colliding headlong into Justin's chest.

'Great catch,' said Jenny.

'Are you okay?' Justin bent his knees to bring himself to Tabbie's eye level.

'Yes. I'm so sorry. It's these wellingtons. They're not mine. Did I hurt you?'

'He's built like a tanker. It'll take more than a damsel in distress to hurt him.'

'I'm fine, thanks.' Justin threw Jenny a sarcastic smile.

'I hope you don't mind me asking,' Jenny said, 'but why were you standing outside in the rain?'

'Oh. I got my boot caught in the mud.'

'I see. I'm Jenny. Jenny Lake. You must be Tabbie. Lovely to meet you at last. How's your car?' Jenny smiled at her.

'A write-off. Did you say, Jenny Lake?'

Jenny gave Justin an apologetic look. 'Yeah. And by the look on your face you've clearly put two and two together. No one was supposed to know. Sorry Justin.'

Justin shrugged. 'Don't worry about it. It was bound to come out sooner or later. But I'd really appreciate it if you wouldn't tell anyone, Tabbie. I wanted to take a short break and also to help out a friend. The last thing I want is to flood this village with paparazzi and the like. It's a lot to ask, I suppose, but can we count on your discretion?'

So Justin Lake had a wife. A wife he kept hidden in his home village. A wife who still ran their bakery.

Breaking that news would be a real sensation – and a major boost for her blog, *Tabbie Talbaine's Tasty Titbits*. She could see the headline now.

'I'll make it worth your while,' Justin added. 'Please Tabbie. You'd be doing me a massive favour. And Jenny too. The last thing she wants is to be bombarded with questions about me.'

'Please, Tabbie,' Jenny pleaded. 'This is such a tiny, tranquil village. It would be ruined if the media heard Justin was here.'

Tabbie knew what it was like to have the media intruding into one's private life. But unlike herself and her mother, Justin wanted fame and fortune. Didn't press coverage go hand and hand with that? Both good and bad. Wasn't that all part and parcel of the Hollywood lifestyle?

But why was his wife content to stay in this village when Justin was in L.A. living life to the full? And from the things Tabbie had read about him, loving several women in the process.

'I have a blog. A fairly popular one. It's called *Tabbie Talbaine's Tasty Titbits*. I write about anything and everything that interests me and may interest my readers and I add a recipe or two and some bits of gossip.'

Neither Jenny or Justin looked happy.

'So what you're saying is you're going to post about this because it's far too good an opportunity to miss. Is that it?' Justin definitely wasn't pleased.

'No. You're correct though. It is a fabulous scoop. And one it's going to be incredibly hard for me not to write about. But I know what it's like to face unwanted media attention and you did come to my rescue and extract my car from its watery grave. I'll admit it's killing me to say this, but I'll make you a deal. If you give me an interview for my blog and let me have some gossip that no one else knows about you, I won't say where we were when you gave me the interview and I won't mention this village or this bakery or Jenny.'

Both Jenny and Justin looked astonished.

'That's it? You don't want anything else?'

Tabbie shook her head. 'That's it. But you'd better be quick before I change my mind.'

'Justin. For heaven's sake. Agree to do it.'

'Okay. It's a deal.'

Tabbie was probably going to regret this. But Jenny and Justin were happy. Although not as ecstatic as Tabbie would have expected. Jenny merely slapped him on the arm and Justin pulled a face at her. Strange behaviour for a husband and wife whose secret had just been preserved.

'Good. Then perhaps we could meet later today and get started on the interview. In the meantime, I'd like two of your coffee-iced cream buns please, Jenny. They come highly recommended. Gill says they're to die for.'

'I don't know about that but they are pretty good, if I do say so myself. And you can put your purse away. They're my treat. It's the least I can do to say thank you.'

'And what about if I cook you dinner tonight?' Justin offered. 'I would buy you dinner at the pub but it's a bit noisy in there to do an interview. I'll pick you up at seven.'

'Oh. If that's all right with Jenny, that would be lovely.'

Jenny shrugged. 'It's fine with me. And he's a good cook, not just a brilliant baker. Oh, and a fantastic actor, of course.' Jenny handed her a box. 'And it's stopped raining again for a while by the looks of it, so that's more good news.'

'I'll dash off then before it starts again. I'll see you at seven.'

'Have fun,' Jenny said, as Justin held the door open for Tabbie to pass. 'I hope I'll see you again soon.'

That was a strange thing to say because surely they'd be seeing each other at dinner?

# Chapter Nineteen

Little Pond Farm was nothing like Tabbie had expected and as they approached the Georgian farmhouse via the long drive, the surprise of seeing such a grand house, having spent the day walking around a village packed with thatched cottages and flower-filled gardens straight from a chocolate box cover, actually made her gasp.

Justin smiled. 'It's a beautiful house, isn't it?'

'And so unexpected. I thought it would be smaller. And older. I think I was expecting it to be of a similar ilk to the rest of the village.'

'This house was built on the site of a Tudor farmhouse, which was destroyed by fire but there's been a farm here since the Iron Age, it's believed. When Jet and I were small kids there was an archaeological dig just yards from the house, over there by the pond.' He nodded towards the field to their left. 'They found traces of a Roman villa, built on an even earlier Iron Age settlement, but not enough was discovered to warrant preservation. Jet's got a map and documents giving more details. He'll show them to you when he gets back, if you're interested.'

She was definitely interested. Who wouldn't be? But Jet wasn't back for another week and she would probably have returned home to London by then.

'I'd love to see them, but I'm not sure I'll be here by the time he gets back.'

'Oh? You're not sticking around then?'

She shook her head. 'No. Only until Gill and I finish our research and we're making such good progress that I don't think it'll be many more days until I have everything I need.'

'Lucky you.' He grinned at her as they pulled up outside the porticoed entrance. 'Very few people have everything they need.'

She smiled. 'I meant in relation to the project I'm working on. I'm writing a blog about witches, and one witch in particular, Jennet de Witt.'

'Aurelia's ancestor? And Aurelia knows about this?'

'Yes. Why does that surprise you?'

He shook his head as he got out of the car and when he held open her door for her his expression was thoughtful.

'I suppose it's because for as long as I've known her, Aurelia's always shunned attention. Of any sort. Half the village forgets she's there most of the time – and that's because she prefers it that way. She keeps herself to herself and if she didn't love fresh milk, and hadn't become addicted to Jet's cheese, I don't think many of us would see her from one year to the next. She doesn't even like people popping in to visit. Unless they've been invited.' He smiled. 'Which doesn't happen often, believe me.'

'Gosh. So my arrival must have turned her world upside down. No wonder she was rather unpleasant to me – until she realised who I was. But she can't always have been like that. She and my mother are friends and many years ago, long before I was born, they were very close. They were both student nurses at Guy's Hospital in London so Aurelia can't have been a hermit in those days. My mother wouldn't have let her.'

Justin looked surprised as they walked towards the house. He opened the large, black front door which led into an expansive hall with an ornate chandelier in the centre. It was an impressive entrance but Tabbie had seen entrances far superior to this in her time. What struck her about this one was that a feeling of warmth swept over her, not from the heat of the fire she could see burning in the large hearth in the sitting room to her left, but as a sensation. A welcome feeling. As if the house itself had given her a hug.

'I don't know what she was like back then,' Justin said, 'and I didn't know she'd trained as a nurse. But she's been this way since I was old enough to talk. To be honest, when she called and asked us to get your car out of her pond, we were surprised to find she hadn't done away with you. Here, let me take your coat.'

'You're joking of course. Aren't you?'

He nodded. 'Yeah. Although …'

Tabbie laughed as she took off her new raincoat – one of the many items she'd purchased only hours earlier. She hadn't planned to be staying in Little Pondale and therefore hadn't brought a change of clothes and since her rescue, she'd either been wearing clothes lent to her by Aurelia, or the clothes she'd worn the day she arrived. But as they had been washed and dried and re-worn twice already, she was beginning to think that a shopping expedition was in order.

Justin's sudden invitation to dinner had solidified that thought and she had dashed to the nearest town, which was half an hour away by minicab, and bought the raincoat, a couple of dresses, two pairs of jeans, three blouses, one skirt and – in case June ever did hit the temperature it should while she was here, a pair of shorts.

Two pairs of sandals, a handbag, some items of make-up and a few pieces of jewellery added to her haul and by the time she had finished she had so many bags that she could hardly carry them to Witt's Cottage, the cab driver having dropped her off where he had picked her up: at the junction of Seaside Road and Aurelia's private lane – if one could call it that.

'There's no way on God's Earth you're getting a cab up that mud track, love,' she'd been told by the cab company she called, as Aurelia had already warned her. 'We'll pick you up on Seaside Road and that's where any cab you call, will also drop you off. Take it from me, love, there ain't enough dough in the whole of Italy to persuade anyone otherwise.'

Quite what dough or Italy had to do with it, Tabbie had no idea, but the cab company she had telephoned, after searching for one via the internet, was called Carlotta's Cabs so perhaps the owners were of Italian origin.

The courtesy car from her insurance company still hadn't arrived by the time she returned to Witt's Cottage and frankly, she was beginning to wonder if it ever would.

'Wow!' Justin said, his eyes alight with obvious admiration. 'You look amazing.'

'Thank you.'

She felt amazing. It was good to get dressed up once in a while and since her break-up with her last boyfriend she hadn't really done that. She'd tried to keep herself busy writing, researching and reading and on the few occasions she had gone out, she had either been with close friends, or her mother, so her outfits had been more casual and her make-up minimal. But she had wanted to make more of an effort for this dinner. After all, it wasn't every day that she was invited to dine with a Hollywood star and his wife. Although she had dined with several minor celebrities.

She'd actually been both a little surprised and disappointed when Justin had turned up at Aurelia's door looking smart but casual. His black trousers were clearly designer but they were daywear, not formal, and his pale lilac shirt was cotton and definitely casual. Expensive without a doubt but again, not a garment she was expecting a star like Justin Lake to wear.

But what had she been expecting? This wasn't a date, after all. It wasn't as if he needed to impress her either. Perhaps this was how he dressed when he was at home.

And that had caused her to panic. Was she overdressed? What would his wife be wearing? Was her tight-fitting, crimson silk, low cut dress too much? She had been careful to make sure the dress was not too low cut, especially with her generous cleavage, but she assumed Jenny would look stunning, what with her wild red hair and incredible bone structure, and Tabbie had wanted to at least hold her own.

'This way,' he said, after hanging her coat in the cloakroom. 'I'd planned for us to eat in the kitchen but I've just realised that was a mistake. Come through to the sitting room and I'll get you a drink while I rearrange a couple of things.'

There was an odd inflection in his tone, almost as if he'd been taken by surprise.

But in a way, so had she. She certainly hadn't expected Justin and his wife to entertain guests in their kitchen. Perhaps they didn't think of her as a guest. That must be it. And she wasn't really, was she? This wasn't a dinner as such. This was merely part of a deal. A deal they'd been forced into by her in exchange for her being willing to keep their secret. She suddenly felt awkward and embarrassed. And she definitely was overdressed. That much was now apparent.

'Oh. Please don't go to any trouble on my account. I ... I'm more than happy to eat in the kitchen.'

'Na-huh.' He shook his head and his eyes travelled the length of her body. 'There's no way you're eating in the kitchen dressed like that. It's a mess. I'm a good cook, but a messy one. It won't take a second and it's really not a problem. It'd make me feel happier too, so please don't argue. Take a seat. Would you like a cocktail, a glass of sherry, wine? No wait. Champagne. That dress demands champagne.'

Her cheeks were rapidly matching the colour of her dress and she quickly sat down and lowered her eyes to the floor. 'Justin, please. This is so embarrassing.'

'Embarrassing? Why? You look gorgeous. I'm the one who should feel embarrassed for not making more of an effort. I should never have expected you to eat in the kitchen. Although it is a pretty posh kitchen.' He grinned at her as she met his eyes but he was clearly disconcerted. 'I don't know what I was thinking.'

'No. It's me. It's my fault. I thought ... I don't know what I thought. I suppose it's because you're a Hollywood star.' She gave an awkward laugh.

He had stopped in the doorway and now he tilted his head to one side.

'Oh I see. I think.'

'Why don't we let Jenny decide where we eat? If she prefers the kitchen, that's honestly fine with me. Really it is.'

'Jenny?' He looked confused. 'Jenny's not joining us.'

'Oh.'

A beeper went off in the distance.

'That's the timer.' He glanced over his shoulder, a perplexed expression on his face as if he wanted to say something more but wasn't sure whether to or not. 'Um. I'd better go and see to it.'

Why wasn't Jenny joining them?

This got more humiliating by the second. She wasn't joining them because this was meant to be a working dinner where Justin was giving an interview he didn't really want to give. Jenny clearly valued her privacy even more than Tabbie had realised.

Tabbie was beginning to wish the floor would open up and swallow her.

It was now emphatically clear that she was not only overdressed; she had completely misread the situation. Jenny and Justin had not invited her to dinner to 'be nice' or 'friendly'. They invited her to dinner to get the deal they had made over and done with. That was it. Nothing more.

But when Justin returned a couple of minutes later, he smiled as he handed her a glass of champagne.

'Cheers,' he said, raising his glass in the air. 'Here's to a pleasant, if somewhat surprising evening. Dinner's ready, and I've hastily set the table in the dining room. Shall we?'

'Cheers,' she replied. 'Yes, of course.'

She stood and followed him to the dining room where two candles in beautifully etched crystal holders had been lit between two place settings across from one another on the large dining table. The lights had been dimmed but not enough to cause her concern. Just enough to give an ambiance.

A bolt of lightning and a crack of thunder made her jump.

'They said a storm was coming,' Justin said, holding her chair for her to sit.

'It's as dark as night out there and it's not even eight yet. Do you mind if I record our conversation? For my blog. I won't use all of it obviously and I'll send you a copy of what I write before I hit the publish button to give you a chance to comment on anything you don't like.'

'Sure. If that helps you, it's okay with me, I guess.'

She smiled and took out the pocket-sized Dictaphone she always carried with her and put it on the table near her glass.

Rain lashed the windows and they rattled against the onslaught.

'That's something I really miss when I'm in L.A. The good old British weather.'

'I'd exchange Britain for L.A. in a heartbeat.'

'Would you? I thought I would too but having been back here for a few weeks now, I think I'll find it quite difficult to return to the bright lights and the arid nights.'

'Well, of course. That's completely understandable.'

'Is it?' He headed back to the door. 'Some people think fame and fortune is the be all and end all and I suppose I was probably one of them this time last year. But there are more important things in life. Like friends and family and being surrounded by people you know and love and trust. I've made friends in L.A. but they're not the same as my friends here.'

'Naturally. But now you're a star, you don't have to live in L.A. full time, do you?'

He shrugged. 'Not really. But my agent thinks I should until I've got a few films under my belt. Until I'm really established. Fame can be fleeting, you know. I'll be back in a sec.'

He was. He placed two large bowls of mushroom and asparagus risotto on the table, a large bowl of fresh mixed salad leaves, a dish of parmesan and a basket of divine-smelling, freshly baked bread, together with the large pepper grinder that had been stuffed beneath his arm.

'Buon appetito,' he said, taking his seat.

'This looks delicious. Risotto is one of my favourite dishes. And is that truffle?'

He beamed at her. 'Mine too. I hope you like it. And yes. What's a good risotto without shaved truffle on the top?'

She took a small mouthful and savoured the flavour and texture.

'Oh Justin. It's divine.'

'I use Carnaroli rice instead of the more frequently used Arborio. It's slightly firmer due to its higher starch content, and it's a little longer.' He laughed suddenly. 'God. I sound like I'm trying to impress you with my knowledge, but I'm not. I remembered you saying that you have recipes on your blog, so I thought you might like this one.'

'It's perfect. I should've taken a photo for the blog.'

'Take one of mine. I haven't touched it yet.'

She whipped out her phone from her bag and took a few shots.

'May I take a couple of you too, please?'

'To use on the blog?'

She nodded. 'If that's okay.'

He shrugged. 'I guess so. With the proviso that you don't say where the photo was taken.'

'Agreed. I'll simply say something like, 'Taken in a dining room at a secret location.' Would that be okay?'

'Perfect.'

Their conversation over dinner flowed naturally. Justin talked honestly and openly about growing up in Little Pondale, about wanting to become a dancer but becoming a baker like his father instead, and how it was Mattie Ward, Mia's great aunt who gave him the confidence to pursue his dream of dancing before an audience when he started The Frog Hill Hounds. Although he did love baking too. How he'd got his big break because someone had seen one of his shows, and how life in Hollywood, as wonderful as it was, still didn't somehow compare to life in Little Pondale. He talked of his lifelong friendship with Jet Cross, whose house this was, and how Jet's relationship with Mia had totally changed Jet's life and brought out the man Jet really was.

'That's the thing about True Love,' Justin said, as they moved from the dining room back to the sitting room for coffee and brandy. 'Some people say Jet's changed. But he hasn't changed deep down. His life has but he hasn't. Deep down, Jet was always the man he now is. He'd simply tried to keep his 'real' self, his 'true' self, hidden so that he wouldn't get hurt, like his mum Sarah had, or hurt anyone like his dad had. True Love brings out the best in people. It doesn't try to change them. But that's just my opinion. And sometimes I talk a lot of crap.'

Tabbie sat on the sofa and to her surprise, Justin sat beside her, close enough that she could smell a subtle hint of sandalwood and lemon, either from his shampoo, soap or aftershave. An image of him in the shower popped into her head and it sent a wave of warmth through her body not unlike the way the brandy was warming her throat, only several times more intense.

She gave a small cough and emptied her glass which she placed on the console table beside her.

'No you don't, Justin. You make a lot of sense and I completely agree with you about True Love. I've simply never been lucky enough to find it. Unlike Jet. And you, of course.'

The one thing Justin had not talked about at all, was his wife.

He was pouring them coffee from the pot on the tray he'd carried in but he stopped, twisted slightly on the sofa cushion and looked her in the eye.

'Me?' He shook his head. 'As I said. Sometimes I talk a lot of crap. I've never found True Love. Perhaps we're not all lucky enough to get it.'

'What about Jenny?'

'Jenny?' He looked thoughtful but also a bit confused. 'Not as far as I know. At least not until now. I suppose this relationship could be it. We'll have to wait and see.'

'Oh. So it's a pretty new one?' That surprised her.

He nodded. 'Since last Christmas.' He finished pouring the coffee and he handed her a cup.

No wonder he didn't want to return to L.A. He and Jenny had only been together since Christmas. A whirlwind romance and a wedding. Gosh. But why was he saying he didn't know if either of them felt True Love? Why did they marry if they weren't sure it would be forever?

Another clap of thunder, immediately overhead this time, made her jump and her cup flew up, sending an arc of liquid into the air which unfortunately landed on the front of Justin's shirt.

'Oh Gosh! I'm so sorry. I've got a tissue in my bag.'

She hastily put the cup and saucer on the table and grabbed a tissue as he held the wet patch of cotton away from his body with his finger and thumb. He was smiling as she dabbed at the brown stain.

'Don't worry about it.'

'I think I'm making it worse.'

He laughed. 'Honestly, Tabbie. It doesn't matter. I'll nip upstairs and throw on something else. I'll only be a sec.'

He got up and walked towards the door as more thunder crashed and lightning lit up the room which, until then was only dimly lit by the flickering flames of the fire and a couple of table lamps dotted here and there.

No one would ever believe it was June. The massive six-over-six windows rattled as yet more rain lashed the glass and wide rivulets cascaded down each pane. She got up and walked to one of the windows, peering out into the darkness where in the distance the one or two trees she could see bent over so far under the whipping wind that the tops of the branches nearly touched the ground.

'This is one hell of a storm,' Justin said, making her jump yet again.

'Gosh. You were quick. Yes. The trees are bowing and almost bent double by the force of the wind. I'm not looking forward to going out in this. Or to you having to drive me back to Witt's Cottage. Perhaps I should call a cab.'

She wasn't looking forward to that prospect either. A cab would mean she'd have to walk up the little lane. In the dark. In this weather. She'd probably end up like her car. Head first in a ditch. Pond. Whatever.

He came and stood beside her, now wearing a plain light grey T-shirt that brought out the colour of his eyes.

'Don't be silly. You're certainly not calling a cab. They won't take you to the door. As for me driving you home, let's see what happens, shall we? The night is still young.'

She glanced at her watch. It was eleven-thirty. Good God! Where had the evening gone? She had been enjoying Justin's company so much that she'd lost all track of time. But she couldn't ask him to take her home right now. As he said, they'd have to wait and see what happened. Although what alternative was there?

Unless he was suggesting that she could possibly stay the night. It was a large house and clearly had several bedrooms but what would Jenny think of that? And where was Jenny? Had she been upstairs all evening? Or was she out somewhere? In which case, why wasn't Justin concerned about his wife getting home safely?

'More brandy?' he asked. 'Or more coffee?' He grinned at that part.

'I'm fine, thank you.'

'I can't argue with that.'

She looked him in the eye. What had that meant? There was something about the way he was looking at her. It sent a bolt through her body not dissimilar to the lightning shooting across the sky and when he took her hand in his, there was definitely more than a spark of electricity. His other arm slid around her waist and she felt her body move towards his.

'Justin,' she said, in a voice unfamiliar to her, and one that couldn't seem to finish her sentence.

His voice sounded different too. Slightly hesitant but oh so tantalisingly sexy and his eyes held hers as his arm tightened about her waist.

'I've been getting mixed messages all evening, so I'm not sure if this is what you want or not, but one thing I am sure of is that I want you, Tabbie Talbaine. I want you a lot.'

'Justin.'

Why couldn't she say anything more? And why did that sound like she wanted him too? It was meant to warn him off. What was wrong with her?

She felt his lips on hers before she realised he had moved in to kiss her.

And God what a kiss.

Forget the storm outside. There was one going on inside her. And it was a hurricane. A Tornado. A–

'Justin! No.'

She managed to break free but it took a second or two to steady herself.

He looked as if she'd slapped his face, but she hadn't. Had she?

Oh dear God. She had. There were thin red lines on his cheek. She could see them when the lightning flashed.

'Okay,' he said. His voice was calm but utterly confused. 'Now that message was clear.'

'I didn't mean to strike you. I'm sorry.'

He brushed his cheek. 'It was a bit of a surprise, but it's fine. You could've simply said, no though. I'm not the kind of guy who would ever step over the line. Perhaps I should've asked if I could kiss you. Not just gone ahead and done it. Sorry. It won't happen again.'

'Why did you?'

'Kiss you?'

'Yes.'

'Because I've been wanting to all evening. Because I think you're beautiful and sexy and hot as hell. Sorry. Inappropriate, I guess. Because I'm attracted to you and I thought you felt the same.'

'I ... I do.' She hadn't meant to say that. 'I'm very attracted to you.' What was she doing? 'I was from the minute I saw you and all those things you said about me, I think about you.' For God's sake woman. *Shut up*!

'Now I really am confused. Is this some sort of game?'

'Not to me. Is it to you?'

'I don't play games with women. Well, not the sort of game we seem to be in now.'

'I don't play games either.'

He shook his head. 'Really? You say you're attracted to me *after* you've slapped my face. Er. You're not into that sadomasochistic sex stuff, are you? Because that's really not my scene.'

'What? No I am not. Slapping your face was an instinctive reaction, I think. I dislike people who cheat on their partners, especially if they're married.'

'Um. What's that got to do with me kissing you?'

'Justin! It's got everything to do with it. You're married!'

He blinked several times.

'No, I'm not.'

'What? Yes you are.'

He smiled sardonically. 'I think I would know if I was married. I've been pretty drunk on several occasions, I'll admit. But even so, I'd remember if I'd married someone.'

'But … Okay. So you just live together and she uses your name. That's just as bad. That's still cheating.'

'Who uses my name? Has someone told you I'm living with them?'

'Jenny! You're living with Jenny.'

For a moment he didn't react but then he burst out laughing as another crack of thunder shook the panes and the expanse of sky behind him lit up like day.

'No, Tabbie. I am not. Most definitely not. Jenny's my cousin. I wondered why you kept mentioning her. It actually crossed my mind that you might … well, that you might be interested in her too, let's just say.'

Tabbie gasped. And blushed. And cringed at her own stupidity.

Why had she jumped to conclusions? Why hadn't it even occurred to her for one second that Jenny and Justin might be related? Because she'd seen him helping Jenny with her hair? And swinging her around in his arms? What was wrong with that? Two things that friends or relatives would do.

'I don't know what to say, Justin. I've been a total idiot. I didn't even think. I should've simply asked. I'm sorry. Can you ever forgive me? And that slap! Oh, Justin, I'm mortified. If I could turn back the clock and start this evening again – this day again, I would. I'm truly sorry.'

'If I reach out and take your hand, will you slap me again?' He was smiling and his voice was tender.

'No. Definitely not.'

He took her hand and again the spark of electricity made her tingle.

'You said if you could turn back the clock, you would. What about if we agree to turn it back to, oh, let's say, that kiss? Would that be okay with you?'

She looked into his eyes and liked what she saw there.

'That would be more than okay. That would be wonderful.'

He slid an arm around her waist and eased her closer as another crack of thunder made the windows shudder.

'Just to make sure there're no mixed messages, or misunderstandings between us let me say this. I'm not married, or living with anyone and my last relationship ended last October. I've been on a few dates since then but that's all. I've wanted to kiss you all evening and, until that slap, I thought it was going pretty well. Oh, and for the sake of clarity, I'm wishing more than anything that this storm gets worse and that you'll have to stay the night, but you'll have your own room unless you tell me you want to sleep in my bed. I don't think I can be clearer than that.' He gave a quick burst of laughter. 'And people say romance is dead. I can be far more romantic, believe me, but I really don't want to get slapped. But seriously, Tabbie. I meant it when I said I think you're beautiful and sexy and hot as hell. And I'm going to kiss you again now, if that's okay. But I won't until you say yes.'

She smiled up at him. 'For the sake of clarity – and romance, I'll say right now that whether or not the storm gets worse, I'd love to spend the night. And I won't be needing my own room because I definitely want to sleep in your bed. You're gorgeous and sexy and hot as hell and if you don't kiss me soon, I *will* slap you because there's nowhere else I want to be than in your arms all night. So yes, Justin. Oh yes.'

# Chapter Twenty

More than a week had passed since Tabbie had spent her first night with Justin, and they had slept together every night since. She had even gone to watch him at rugby training, and joined everyone at The Frog and Lily afterwards for drinks. She and Justin had not stayed long at the pub though. They had raced back to Little Pond Farm and tumbled into bed, hardly able to restrain themselves on the seemingly long drive to the farmhouse, which in reality was only a matter of five minutes. Probably less, the way Justin was driving.

Tabbie had no inclination to go home to London. She had not replaced her car and, despite constant assurances, the courtesy car had still not turned up. Aurelia insisted that she was welcome to stay at Witt's Cottage for as long as she liked and as her mother was away with friends, there was really no reason for Tabbie to leave.

But there was a very good reason for her to stay.

It had been a long time since she had felt this way about a man.

Had she ever felt this way?

She had certainly never been so eager to see anyone as she was to see Justin. Five minutes after they said goodbye, she was counting the minutes until she could be in his arms again.

She giggled to herself, remembering something he had said. She tingled at the thought of his touch; sighed at the memory of their last kiss. And actually made a sound resembling the squeal of an overly excited piglet when her mind wandered back to the last time they had made love. As they were hardly ever apart, they made love rather a lot.

But she did feel a little guilty for not spending much time at Aurelia's since that first night with Justin. The pair of them had dinner with Aurelia at Witt's Cottage one evening, and Tabbie popped in briefly each day, either for morning coffee or afternoon tea, but other than that, her time and attention was taken up with Justin, morning, noon and night. She even helped out on the farm, much to the surprise and delight of Franklin and Pete. She had not seen much of Gill, but since he and Ella had got engaged, Gill seemed far less interested in research than he had been, so he clearly didn't mind. But she did not want Aurelia to think that she had abandoned her project.

'I'm sorry I haven't been around much,' she said, handing Aurelia a large piece of cheese she had brought with her from Little Pond Farm. 'I know it's rather discourteous of me and I apologise for that. But whatever this is with Justin feels so good, so wonderful, so right that I want to be with him every minute of every day, as crazy as that sounds. I hope you don't think I'm ignoring you.'

Aurelia smiled and squeezed Tabbie's hand after taking the cheese and putting it on the table. 'Don't give it another thought. I don't think any such thing. I'm glad you're having a good time and it doesn't sound crazy at all. What would be crazy would be to spend time with an old lady like me when you can be in the arms of such a gorgeous young man. Make the most of it, my dear. We never know what's around the corner.'

'That's sounds ominous. Do you know something I don't?'

'Don't look so worried, Tabbie. It's just a saying.' She went to the Aga and took a freshly baked loaf of bread out of the oven, placing it on the table beside the cheese. 'I can't see into the future. I'm a healer and an enabler – or a witch if you prefer, but I'm not a fortune-teller.'

Tabbie breathed in the wonderful aroma. Was that lavender she could detect in that loaf?

Aurelia added, 'If knowing what lies ahead is what you want, you'll need my sister for that. She's the fortune-teller in the family. She'll be here in August, as usual.'

'A fortune-teller? You have a sister? I didn't know that.'

Aurelia tapped her nose. 'There're a lot of things you don't know, my dear. Half the skill in having a happy life is knowing what it is you don't know in the present and making sure you do know in the future.'

Tabbie thought about that for a moment.

'I now know you have a sister and that she'll be here in August. What I don't know is why you haven't mentioned her before, what her name is, whether she's older or younger and why she only comes in August. Oh. And if she is your only sister? Sorry. If she is your only sibling? Gill and I hadn't got that far with our research into your family tree.'

Aurelia smiled. 'You're a quick learner, Tabbie Talbaine. Just like your dear mother. Cami soon learnt … but we were talking about you and Justin.'

'No. We were talking about you and your sister. Don't think you can change the subject and expect me not to notice.'

Aurelia laughed. 'My younger sister's name is Jezebella. She comes here for Christmas and my birthday, but other than that she's here in August, for the annual Summer Fête. Which is why she ran off in the first place, more than thirty years ago. Fell in love, she did. Pity she hadn't thought to tell her own fortune beforehand. But it's unlucky to do that, so it's said. Things didn't work out as she had hoped. She loves life on the road though, so she spends her summers telling fortunes, and her winters in Tenerife. She's got a little white-washed house in a fishing village, right by the sea. I've been there once or twice.'

'Gosh. That's a surprise. Tenerife? How lovely. Aren't you tempted to move there too? Or at least spend the winters there.'

Aurelia looked shocked. 'Why would I do that? I'm happy where I am. But let's forget about Jezebella. I'd much rather talk about Justin. What don't you know about him that you know you need to know?'

'Oh. I think he's been completely honest and upfront with me about himself. We've spent a great deal of time talking, not just …'

A broad grin crept across Aurelia's wizened face. 'I was young once, dear. And if I were young right now, I wouldn't spend much of my time talking to Justin. Oh no. We could talk when we got old.'

Tabbie laughed. 'I love talking with Justin, almost as much as anything else. I want to get to know him. Although the strange thing is, from the very first time we kissed, I felt as if I'd known him all my life. I'm well aware that's a cliché, but it's true. Well, actually no. Not the very first time. That time I did feel something but it was so tainted with guilt and shock that I slapped him. It was from the second time.'

'You slapped Justin? That's the first I've heard of that.'

By the time Tabbie had finished telling Aurelia about the misunderstanding, Aurelia was holding her stomach as if she had a stitch.

'That'll be a story for the grandchildren.'

'Grandchildren? Gosh. I wish.' Tabbie let out a sigh. 'Are you sure you can't see into the future?'

'Absolutely certain. There's something else you need to know then, isn't there?'

'About Justin? Or about our relationship? I know that too. As I said, he's been open and honest from the start. He's got to return to L.A. This is just a holiday romance. It'll last for as long as we're both in Little Pondale.'

'Is that what he says?'

'Not in those words, but yes.'

'Is that why you're still here? Not that I want you to leave, because I don't.'

Tabbie sighed again. 'In a way, yes. But also because Gill and I haven't finished our research. Since he and Ella got engaged, and Justin and I got together, we haven't seemed to be able to find much time when we're both free to continue.'

'Do you want to continue?'

'Yes. It's fascinating. But not quite as fascinating as Justin.' Tabbie smiled and slipped an arm around Aurelia's shoulders. 'Gill still wants to find the right map for his neighbour, although he says he can't tell me why because Hettie specifically asked him not to but–'

'Hettie? Hettie Turner? What kind of map?'

'A map of Little Pondale. As I said, I don't know which map or why, only that's it's of the village and the surrounding area, and that she's not looking for treasure or anything. Just some sort of natural phenomenon or something. I think it has something to do with water.'

'Is she indeed?' Aurelia's shoulder stiffened beneath Tabbie's hand. 'I know exactly what Hettie Turner is looking for. What I don't know is why? And that is something I know I need to know.'

# Chapter Twenty-One

'Please don't get upset,' Ella said.

She had been sitting rather comfortably on Hettie's new sofa but now she was perched on the edge, squeezing Hettie's hand in one of hers while Fred grabbed the brandy bottle and Gill raced to the kitchen to get a glass.

'I can't wait for a glass. Hand me the bottle, Fred.'

Fred did as asked and Hettie swigged down two large gulps before Gill returned.

'Too late,' Justin said, hovering nearby as if he wasn't quite sure what to do, other than hold Tabbie in a comforting hug.

'I'm so, so sorry, Hettie.' Tabbie was mortified. But clearly unsure what she had done to warrant such a telling off from Hettie.

Ella shot a warning look at Tabbie and mouthed the word, 'Shush.' What she really wanted to say was, 'For God's sake woman will you shut up. Haven't you done enough already by almost giving poor Hettie a seizure.' But she didn't say that. Partly because it wouldn't help and partly because Justin would be furious.

It was pretty obvious to her – and no doubt everyone else in the village, that Tabbie and Justin were besotted with each other. He'd told Gill that it was just for whatever time they had together before returning to their own lives, but Ella wasn't convinced. Justin had never looked at her in quite the same way as he looked at Tabbie and she wasn't sure whether she was happy for them both or just a little bit annoyed that when they were dating Justin hadn't found her as appealing as he apparently found Tabbie.

'I don't know what you were thinking, deary.' Hettie still grasped the neck of the brandy bottle in one hand as she glared at Tabbie. 'And as for you, Guillaume. I thought I'd made it clear that this was our little secret. For a man who's written a book about his grandfather's life in the French Resistance, you've got a thing or two to learn about the importance of keeping your mouth shut. Loose lips cost lives, deary.'

'I'm sorry, Hettie. There isn't much more I can say. Except that the idioms you were looking for are "Loose lips might sink ships" and "Careless talk cost lives". They were part of the ... I'm not doing myself any favours by telling you that, am I?'

'No, deary. You're not.' Hettie took another swig from the bottle and handed the bottle to Fred.

'But what's done is done and can't be undone. Don't even think about correcting me.' She glowered at Gill.

He raised his hands in the air. 'I wasn't even considering it.'

'Hmm. So where's the map?'

Gill gave Ella a pleading look.

'We don't have it,' Ella said. 'Yet. But we will, Hettie. I promise you. But the fact you were looking for the map wasn't really a secret, was it, because you told me and Cathy? The only secret is why you want it. And none of us knows that. So it's still a secret, isn't it? And Mia and Jet will be home tomorrow.'

'Hmm. I'm well aware of Mia and Jet's imminent return. I may be old and I may put my trust in the wrong people but I'm not completely barmy. It'll be lovely to have them back but I don't see how that helps me with the map.'

Ella coughed. 'Because, like everyone else in this village, Aurelia has a soft spot for Jet, I believe. And I don't mean the ditch Tabbie drove her car into.'

'Pond. It was a pond … I'll be quiet.'

'I think you should.'

'Ella.' Justin snapped. 'Don't get stroppy with Tabbie. It was your fiancé who told her about the map.'

'I'm standing right here, Justin. And I think I made it clear that it was confidential.'

'Then why did you tell Tabbie about it?'

'Because–'

Fred banged the bottle down onto the coffee table. 'Shut up, everyone. Please. Ella, you were saying something about Aurelia and Jet.'

'Er. Yes.' She glanced from Gill to Justin and shook her head. 'Hettie, Tabbie's already asked for Aurelia's help, and Aurelia won't give it until you tell her why you want the map, which you won't do. So as far as I can see, the only person who may be able to persuade one or both of you to relent, is Jet.'

Hettie crossed her arms beneath her chest and puffed out her cheeks.

'It won't be me. As much as I love our Jet, he'll not make me budge. A secret's called a secret for a reason.'

She glared at Gill once more as if waiting for him to speak, but he merely nodded.

Tabbie raised one hand like a schoolgirl asking for permission.

'Yes,' Ella said, somewhat irritably.

'It won't be Aurelia either. She's adamant that until she knows why Hettie wants it, she won't tell anyone what she knows.'

'Don't shout at me, Hettie,' Gill said, 'but couldn't you just tell Aurelia? You don't have to tell any of us.'

'No.'

'What I don't get,' said Ella, after an awkward silence, and still holding Hettie's hand, 'is the fact that you and Aurelia have lived in this village all your lives. Weren't you ever friends?'

'We were good friends.'

'Oh, I see.'

'No, Ella Swann. You do not.'

Ella's mouth dropped open and she shot a look at Gill who looked as stunned as her.

'Um. I think I do. You obviously had a falling out and because you're both so stubborn, neither of you wants to be the first to apologise.'

Hettie glowered at her and snatched her hand away.

'Sometimes, deary, life is not as simple as you seem to think. I need another glass of brandy, Fred.'

Ella was grateful that Gill didn't try to point out that so far, strictly speaking, having drunk from the bottle, Hettie hadn't had one glass yet.

# Chapter Twenty-Two

July not only brought Mia and Jet back to Little Pondale, it brought sunshine and a temperature of thirty degrees centigrade on its very first day.

'What are you doing?' Mia laughed, as Jet swept her up into his arms after helping her out of the limousine.

'I'm carrying my bride over the threshold of our home.'

She kissed him on the lips as he walked towards the front door, but just as he put his foot on the stone step beneath the portico, the front door burst open and a cacophony of voices yelled, 'Welcome home!'

Jet stumbled and nearly dropped Mia but he managed to regain his footing and held her firmly against his chest.

'Bloody hell,' Mia said, none too happy that she was almost sprawled across the ground and that her husband could've had a heart attack. 'What on earth are you all doing here?'

'We wanted to surprise you,' said Ella, apologetically.

'Mission accomplished,' said Jet, whose lips twitched as he adjusted his hold on his wife. 'But if you'll be good enough to step aside, I have a little mission of my own I'd like to complete. If that's okay with all of you.'

Ella, Gill, Lori, Franklin, Bree, Garrick, Justin, Tabbie and virtually half the village, including Hettie and Fred, Leo, Cathy and Daisy, Christy, Toby and Dylan, Alexia and Bear and Jenny and Glen stepped back into the hall to let Jet pass. Only Little M seemed to think she didn't have to comply with her master's wishes as she rushed to him and leapt up and down excitedly in front of every step he took.

'It's not too late to get back on a plane to paradise, my darling,' he said to Mia.

'I think it is,' she replied, now smiling in response to that grin of his she loved so much.

Jet glanced down at Little M. 'Yes, yes, Little M. We love you too. Er. If you're not too busy, would one of you mind grabbing my dog.'

'Your what?' joked Ella. 'You're not on some hedonistic honeymoon island now you know.' But she grabbed Little M and held her tight.

'Don't I know it,' said Jet.

He finally made it into the hall and gently set Mia down. Then he kissed her passionately in front of the crowd who all cheered and hooted and clapped.

'Welcome home, my darling wife.'

'Welcome home to you, my wonderful husband.'

'Dear God' said Ella. 'You're not going to keep referring to yourselves like that, are you?'

'Yep,' Mia said. 'Get used to it. And next time you plan a surprise welcome home party, please tell me about it. I nearly ended up head first in the gravel.'

'Good thing Jet plays rugby and knows how to hang on to a ball,' Toby said.

'Don't even go there, Ella.' Jet threw Ella a warning look, but he was grinning.

Mia gave Ella a massive hug while Jet gave Little M a big cuddle. Then Mia and Jet switched places.

'You smell of dog,' Ella said, to Jet's chest. 'Sorry. I shouldn't talk about your wife like that.' She laughed as Jet squeezed her tighter. And tighter. 'Er. I can't breathe.'

'Excellent,' said Jet. But he laughed as he let her go, even though she slapped him on his arm.

Lori dashed forward, handed the tray of champagne filled glasses to Ella and pulled Mia close.

'I missed you so much, sweetheart. Was it wonderful? Did you have fun? What was the villa like? Was the place as beautiful as they say?'

'I've missed you too, Mum. And, Yes. Lots. Amazing. More so.' She beamed at Lori. 'I'll tell you everything later.'

'Not everything, I hope.' Jet raised his brows.

Mia gave him a playful tap with her fingers.

'We've got so much to tell you and so many photos. We broke the return journey up and spent nights in Tahiti, Christchurch and Hong Kong. I wanted to go to The Raffles Hotel in Singapore but it's closed for restoration until August, so we went to Hong Kong instead. But it still meant an overnight flight from there and even in a first-class bed, I didn't sleep that well. I've no idea why I'm telling you this now. Basically, I could murder a drink.'

'Here,' said Ella, handing her a glass of champagne. She passed the tray to Gill. 'Hand these around please, oh love of my life.' She grinned and blew him a kiss before grabbing a glass for herself.

'Ella!' Mia screamed, taking her friend's left hand in hers. 'Let me see this ring. I completely forgot for a moment. Blame the jetlag. It's gorgeous. I couldn't believe it when you told us. Congratulations again.'

'Thanks. Sorry we woke you both up so early that day but I couldn't wait to tell you and I forgot the time difference.'

'It was three in the morning,' Jet said, winking. 'But fortunately for you, we were awake. It was our honeymoon, after all.'

'Everybody!' Mia raised her glass. 'Let's all toast to Ella and Gill.'

All glasses were raised and several toasts were made. To Ella and Gill. To Mia and Jet's return. To welcome Tabbie to the village. To the sun coming out. To Bree making a success of her June weddings, despite the appalling weather. The list went on and on.

'So much for a quiet night in on our first day home,' Jet said, kissing Mia. 'But I suppose we'll have lots of those between now and our nineties.'

'Not if we have kids,' Mia said, the one thing she still wished for coming to the front of her mind.

'True. Although we can always stick them in one of the sheds with the animals if we want some alone time.'

'Or get Ella to babysit. She deserves to be punished for this.'

Mia smiled at Jet. He knew how much she wanted a baby. She couldn't hide anything from him. But making light of it didn't stop that odd little pain in her heart, no matter how happy she was.

'I suppose we'd better mingle.'

Jet took her hand in his.

'I suppose we should.'

She held on tight. With Jet by her side, she could face anything. No matter what the future had in store.

# Chapter Twenty-Three

Mia grinned at Jet who was holding a mug of coffee in his right hand and one of Jenny's sticky buns in his left, his head hanging low just above the kitchen table.

'It's the morning after the night before, as the saying goes,' Mia said, to everyone seated around the kitchen table of Little Pond Farm. 'Either he's got a hangover or he's suffering from jetlag. Rather appropriate, given his name.'

Jet lifted his head and gave her one of his grins, only not quite as enthusiastically as he usually did.

He looked at Ella. 'You're seriously telling me that Hettie's looking for some magic water thing and Aurelia knows where it is and won't tell her?'

Ella nodded.

'And you thought bringing me a sticky bun at eleven in the morning, the day after I return from honeymoon, was going to entice me to trek to

Aurelia's and try to persuade her to give up her secrets?'

Ella nodded again.

'Oh good. That's cleared that up. Jesus Christ. People seemed relatively sane when we left, Mia. What on earth's happened to them while we've been away?'

'It rained,' Ella said. 'A lot.'

'And?'

'If it hadn't rained so much, Tabbie would've seen the track to Witt's Cottage and not landed in the ditch-pond-thing.'

'And?'

Ella huffed. 'Tabbie wouldn't have stayed at Aurelia's. She would've popped in, done her video clip for her mum's big day, and hightailed it back to London.'

'Still don't see the connection.'

'She wouldn't have heard Aurelia's stories. Wouldn't have got Gill involved. And wouldn't have blabbed to Aurelia about Hettie wanting a map.'

'Ah.'

'Excuse me,' said Tabbie, nursing her mug of tea. 'That wouldn't change Hettie's situation. Hettie would've still asked Gill to find the map. Eventually, he would've realised that Aurelia might be able to help in some way.'

Jet nodded. 'Tabbie does have a point. But this gets us nowhere. If I say I'll ask Aurelia as soon as I feel half human again, will you all leave and let me crash out on the sofa?'

'I hope that doesn't include me,' Mia said, grinning at him.

'Nope. I want you on the sofa with me.'

Ella tutted. 'The honeymoon's over. Welcome back to our world. So you'll do it?'

Jet slowly nodded.

'Soon?'

'Go away, Ella.'

'Can I at least finish my coffee?'

'If you do it quietly. I'm going outside for some fresh air and I'm taking my cake and my coffee. I may be a while.'

Jet gingerly got to his feet and Little M, who had been lying beside his left foot, jumped up and raced to the door.

'I don't think I've ever seen him like this,' Ella whispered to Mia.

'Nor me.'

'I have,' said Justin, who was still staying at the farmhouse. 'Long time ago though. And I for one am very glad it rained. If it hadn't, this gorgeous woman wouldn't be sleeping beside me each night.' He put an arm around Tabbie and kissed her. 'But I'd better go and do some work. There's no way Jet's going to be fit to do any today and I guess I should continue to earn my keep until I get my marching orders.'

Mia watched as Tabbie blushed and fidgeted in her seat.

Justin clearly realised the importance of his statement and hastily added, 'Which I hope won't be for a while yet. Or I can go and stay with Jenny at the bakery.'

'You're welcome here as long as you like,' Mia reassured him.

His look of relief was palpable.

'Thanks, Mia. I really appreciate that.' He blew Tabbie a kiss and headed for the door to the farmyard.

Gill got up and kissed Ella. 'I'll see if there's anything I can do to help outside. I can tell you girls want to talk.'

'What about you, Tabbie?' Mia asked once Gill had left. 'Are you going to be sticking around? Justin's more than half in love with you and it seems to me you feel the same about him.'

Tabbie nodded. 'I do. But we haven't known each other long and I can't stay at Aurelia's for ever, just as Justin can't stay here. We've both got lives elsewhere. Me in London. Him in L.A. This was merely a sort of holiday fling. Summer Kisses, my mother calls this type of thing.'

'It doesn't mean your relationship has to end,' said Ella.

Tabbie shrugged. 'Maybe not. But long-distance relationships are hard.'

'But worth it if you really love someone.'

'We'll see. I wouldn't mind moving to L.A. to be honest. It's somewhere I've always wanted to live. But I don't want to leave my mother. I've got the basement flat in her house. She's sixty this year and it wouldn't feel right if I upped and left.'

'Sixty is nothing,' Ella said. 'Lori's in her sixties and she's started a whole new life with Franklin. Perhaps your mum feels that she can't leave you. Have you thought of that? Perhaps she'd like to sell the house and move to L.A. or Paris or Bognor. I don't know but you should talk to her. You might be surprised.'

'Your mother does seem blissfully happy,' Tabbie said to Mia. 'Thanks Ella. I'll do that. Even if she says no, at least I'll know.'

'Mum is happier than I've seen her since my dad was alive. But even if she wasn't with Franklin, she wouldn't want me to put my life on hold for her. She'd hate it if she ever thought I'd done that. Your mum feels the same, I'm sure. All mums do. They want their children to be happy. If the children are happy, the mums are happy too.'

'You'll make a wonderful mother, Mia,' Tabbie said.

Mia cleared her throat. 'If it happens. We'll have to wait and see. But there's nothing I'd like more than for me and Jet to have a baby.'

'It'll happen,' Ella said, nudging Mia. 'You've just got to give it time. And speaking of babies and moving, Gill and I have been discussing things and I don't know what you think but Willow Cottage is going to be too small for Bree, Garrick, Flora and the cygnet twins. Cygnet twins. Get it? Baby 'Swanns'. My talent is wasted here.'

'I suppose that's true. Not about your talent, but Willow Cottage is definitely tiny. Are you suggesting Bree and the babies move into Sunbeam Cottage with Garrick and Flora instead of them moving in with her? I hadn't even thought that far ahead.'

'I'm suggesting that perhaps Gill and I should move out.'

'To where? To Willow Cottage? Would you do that? You love Sunbeam Cottage.'

'I do. But it does make sense. Or there is an alternative. Gill's still got his place in Cambridge.'

'You can't move to Cambridge! I couldn't bear it. That's too far away.'

'Some mums don't want to let go of their kids, Tabbie,' Ella joked, rolling her eyes at Mia. 'Do you honestly think I'd move more than ten miles away from you? You're stuck with me for life. What I was going to say was that if Gill sells his place in Cambridge, we might be able to buy somewhere around here when a cottage becomes available but if we could live in Willow Cottage until then, that'd be great.'

'We can buy you somewhere.'

'You've done more than enough for us already. No. We want to do this ourselves.'

'Okay. Then let us at least give you an interest free loan. Like Mattie did for Jet to help him buy this place.'

Ella didn't say no immediately. 'Thank you, Mia. You're such a good friend. We might take you up on that offer.'

'It's there whenever you want it.'

'I wish we knew who owns the cottage next door. The one between Sunbeam and Duckdown. That would be the perfect place to live. Although on second thoughts, Garrick could move in there and Gill and I can stay in Sunbeam. I'd still like some space between me and Hettie, as much as I've grown to love her. She's been acting weird lately though. What with this map malarkey and everything. I'm so glad you're back. Little Pondale just didn't feel right without you and Jet here.'

# Chapter Twenty-Four

Jet tried for two weeks to get Hettie to tell him why she wanted to find the natural spring known as The Witch's Tears, and for Aurelia to give him some indication of where to find it, but even he had no success with either of them.

'I don't know what else I can do,' he told Mia one morning at breakfast. 'They're both behaving like kids. Or worse than kids. I'm tempted to bash their heads together.'

'Maybe that's exactly what you should do.'

'What? I thought you loved me. Do you want me to spend twenty years in jail?'

'No. And you know I love you. But it's not such a bad idea. If we could get them in the same room, face-to-face, one of them would be bound to say something. At least then we'd know why they fell out. Ella told me that Hettie said they were good friends once, so something pretty major must've happened to cause such a rift. And once one said something, the other one might too.

Before you know it, they'll be screaming at one another and eventually, we can hope, they'll calm down and perhaps try to work things out.'

'You're right. That's not such a bad idea. In fact. It's a pretty good one. I even threatened to cut off Aurelia's supply of cheese, and if that didn't work, nothing else will. Perhaps getting them together is our only solution.'

'It's either that or admitting defeat. And I'm not prepared to do that, are you?'

'Absolutely not.' Jet leapt up. 'And there's no better time than the present.'

Mia frowned. 'May I finish my coffee first?'

He kissed the top of her head. 'You may. I'll call Gill and get him to bring Hettie here on some pretext of me having found something amongst my papers that might refer to the spring she's looking for and I'll get Justin to call Aurelia and say that Tabbie needs her here because of something or other. I'll ask Tabbie to think up a believable story. Once both Hettie and Aurelia are here, we can lock them in the dining room and tell them they're staying there until they sort this out.'

'The dining room? I'd better ask Tabbie to give me a hand moving all the breakables then. Do you think either Hettie or Aurelia could lift a chair? I'd hate one of those to get broken.'

Jet grinned as he pressed the button on the landline phone to call Gill.

'Perhaps we should lock them in one of the barns instead.'

He told Gill the plan and a few minutes later, Gill called back. Persuading Hettie to go to Little Pond Farm had not been a problem.

Aurelia, on the other hand, was an entirely different matter. It was almost as if she knew Mia and Jet were trying to trick her.

'She doesn't believe me.' Justin muted the kitchen phone while he told Mia and Jet. 'She says if Tabbie's badly hurt, I should call an ambulance, not her, and if Tabbie isn't, then I should take her to Aurelia's and she'll make up some healing herbs for Tabbie to take, and she'll put her to bed.'

'Please don't ask me to speak to her,' said Tabbie. 'I'm hopeless at telling even the tiniest white lie. No one ever believes me.'

'Will you try, Jet?'

Justin held out the phone to him and Jet put it on speaker.

'Aurelia, hi. This is Jet. Look, I don't know if Tabbie's injury is bad or not. All I know is she's asking for you and she sounds as if she's in pain.' He waved his hand at Tabbie to indicate she should scream.

Mia burst out laughing and had to cover her mouth. Tabbie sounded more like a constipated opera singer than a woman in real pain.

Aurelia sighed long and hard down the phone.

'Tabbie Talbaine, don't ever try to take to the stage. And as for you, Jet Cross, you should be ashamed of yourself. If lying to an old woman is your idea of fun, you're not the man I thought you were.'

Jet sucked in a breath and let it out on a sigh almost as long as Aurelia's.

'I apologise, Aurelia. It seemed like a good idea at the time. I just don't know what else to do to make you two see sense. Mum would've known. And so would Mattie … Aurelia? … Are you still there?'

'Yes, Jet. I'm still here? Very well then. Your dear mother and Mattie both meant a lot to me. If lying is the length you'll go to just so that Hettie Turner can discover where to find The Witch's Tears then so be it. But she might not be happy when she knows the answer. I want to see all of you at Witt's Cottage in half an hour. And that means all of you. Mia and Jet, Tabbie and Justin, and bring Gill and Ella along too. And Hettie Turner. I suppose you'd better bring her husband Fred. But if that rat of hers crosses my threshold, my cats'll have him before he knows what's what, so tell her to leave him at home. Half an hour, or I might change my mind.'

# Chapter Twenty-Five

In the warmth of the July sunshine, the track leading to Witt's Cottage actually looked like a lane, and the overgrown hedges didn't overhang the pond quite so much. The pond itself didn't look so bad either. It no longer resembled a muddy ditch. Mia and Jet, along with everyone Aurelia had stated must be there, arrived in two vehicles and parked far enough away from the pond to avoid any mishaps.

'The water's almost clear now,' Tabbie said, as they walked past the pond. 'And now I can see why the undercarriage of my car was so badly damaged. There definitely are rocks in there. Look.'

'Is it my imagination, or are they sparkling?' Mia asked, holding Jet's hand as she leant over to peer down to the bottom.'

Everyone peered into the pond and nodded.

'It's the sunlight on the water,' Justin said.

'Perhaps it's gold,' said Ella. 'Or jewels. Perhaps there's a treasure after all and Hettie's been telling us all fibs.'

Hettie tutted and backed away from the edge as she held Fred's hand.

'I told you, deary, it's not that sort of treasure. It's water.'

'This is water,' Mia pointed out.

Hettie didn't bother to respond.

'I think it's the minerals in the rocks,' Gill said. 'That's making them sparkle, I mean. Geology wasn't my best subject so I don't know for sure but there are three main types of rock, I believe. Igneous, metamorphic and sedimentary. They all have elements in their composition that might cause them to shine, or sparkle or glisten. But you probably don't need to know that.'

'I do love you, Gill,' Ella said, kissing him on his cheek as they headed towards Witt's Cottage through the small copse.

The garden was in full bloom and myriad flowers swayed in the gentle breeze beneath dappled rays of sunshine. Two cats, one black and jauntily stepping between the flowers, one ginger and curled up on the path, glanced at the approaching entourage, both deciding it did not warrant further investigation and returning to the business at hand of chasing butterflies or sleeping.

Aurelia opened the door and two more cats bounded out into the sunshine.

'Come in,' Aurelia said, glaring at Hettie.

Hettie and Fred went in first, followed by Mia, Jet and the others.

'In there,' Aurelia pointed to the sitting room. 'There's herbal tea, and there's coffee. There's also fresh lemonade. Help yourselves.'

For someone who didn't often have visitors, the sitting room seemed to have a great many chairs, some more comfy than others by the look of them. Mia sat in one near the door, in case she wanted to make a speedy exit. She could see glimpses of the pond and the overgrown hedges through the copse and smiled as a Kingfisher came and perched on a branch overhanging the glistening water.

Jet sat on the arm of her chair and Hettie sat close by with Fred. The others took various seats until everyone including Aurelia was seated.

She nodded to Tabbie and as if Tabbie could read Aurelia's mind, she asked each in turn what they would like and began pouring tea, coffee or lemonade accordingly.

Aurelia sat back in her chair and another black cat leapt onto her lap and made itself comfortable.

'You want to find The Witch's Tears then, do you? And you expect me to tell you where it is without telling me why?'

She didn't look at Hettie but it was obvious the question was directed at her.

'I think it's the least you could do after … well, there's no need for us to rehash the past.

There's something I want and The Witch's Tears may help me get it.'

Aurelia narrowed her eyes. 'What if you make a mistake? Like last time.'

Hettie puffed out her cheeks, clasped her hands together and crossed her arms beneath her bosom.

'I wasn't the one who made the mistake, Aurelia Jenkins.'

'It certainly wasn't me.'

'It must've been one of us and I followed your instructions precisely.'

'Did you? To the letter?'

'Of course I did.'

'Then someone must've intervened.'

'Intervened? Who could've intervened? And why would they?'

'Where was Hector?'

'Hector was …' A look of horror swept across Hettie's face. 'Now look here, Aurelia. Don't you go blaming my Hector for your mistakes.'

'I don't make mistakes, Hettie Turner. I told you then and I'm telling you now. It was you or yours. Not me.'

'I did what you said. Hector's actions shouldn't have made any difference.'

'You or yours, Hettie. You or yours.'

'No. I didn't come for this. Are you going to help me or not? Where is The Witch's Tears?'

Aurelia smiled. 'Only those with a good heart can find The Witch's Tears. You don't think

Jennet would let just anyone benefit from them, do you?'

No one else had said a word or made a sound. Not even Ella. And what surprised Mia almost as much was that Hettie hadn't said the word 'dear' or 'deary' once throughout her entire conversation with Aurelia. It was almost as if Hettie were a different person.

'So you obviously can't see it then?' Hettie glared at Aurelia and Aurelia glared back.

'Ladies,' Jet said. 'This isn't helping. I don't know what happened between you two in the past but clearly something did and it's still influencing your behaviour to this day. Isn't it time to bury the hatchet?'

'I'll bury it in her head,' Hettie said.

'You'd miss and put it in the wrong place.'

Mia shook her head and glanced through the window. They might not find The Witch's Tears but this was going to ends in tears if they carried on like this.

The Kingfisher was still on the branch. He tilted his head to one side as if listening for something then he disappeared into the copse in a blue flash, reappearing a second or two later this side of the trees, just a little to the right of the cottage where the flower filled beds met the wildflowers and hedges surrounding the pond. He landed on yet another overgrown hedge, shook his head and stretched out his colourful wings, his bright blue and orange plumage resplendent in the sunshine.

Mia couldn't take her gaze from him and the cacophony of voices in the sitting room faded into a muffled hum as she watched him. Then something else caught her eye.

It wasn't raining so why was there water trickling down the leaves. Droplets glistened in the sunshine like tiny pear-shaped diamonds. It was so peaceful and magical she wanted to run outside and catch some in her hands. To get out of this room where Hettie and Aurelia flung insults at one another and Jet and the others were trying to get them to stop.

'That's it!' Mia jumped up from her seat, startling everyone in the room, including the little black cat. She looked at Jet, then Hettie and finally Aurelia. 'I think I know where The Witch's Tears is.'

'You do?' Aurelia looked doubtful at first, and then she smiled and nodded and let out a weary sigh. 'You do.'

'You do?' queried Hettie.

'Really?' asked Ella.

'You're sure?' confirmed Jet.

'Yes.' She met Aurelia's eyes. 'It's your ancestor's secret, Aurelia. Hettie must have a good reason to want this, or she wouldn't be here. Whatever happened between you must've been long ago. Can't you send it back where it belongs and move on? Can't you put it behind you? I want to tell Hettie where it is. Is that all right with you?'

Aurelia glanced at Hettie. 'It's not as straightforward as you might think. The Witch's Tears, I mean. Like any spell, it needs great care. You got it wrong before. Whatever it is you want, if you make a mistake, it could have consequences. Terrible consequences.'

'Then I'll have to be sure I don't make a mistake.'

Aurelia nodded. 'Then show her, Mia.' Aurelia turned away and slowly walked towards the door.

'Wait,' Mia said. 'Aren't you going to stay and help? If it's so important that Hettie doesn't get it wrong, she'll need someone to tell her how to do it right. Surely you're the only person who can do that? Won't you do that for someone you once called a friend? If Ella and I ever had a row which tore us apart and years later she needed my help, I know I would give it willingly.'

'Nothing could ever tear us apart,' Ella said. 'But the same goes for me.'

'And for me and Justin,' Jet said. 'And now Gill too. I'd do it for any friend, if they asked.'

'So would I,' said Tabbie.

Aurelia banged her stick on the floor. 'But she hasn't asked.'

'Hettie?' Mia looked at her.

Hettie pursued her lips.

'Go on, love,' Fred said. 'It's time. You let Hector go so that you could let new love in. Can't you let go of this to give friendship a chance to regrow? Before it's too late?'

'Too late?' Aurelia asked. 'Too late for what?'

'None of us is getting any younger,' Hettie said. 'That's all Fred meant.'

Aurelia stepped forward and looked into Hettie's eyes. 'No, Hettie Turner. None of us is getting any younger. But we'll be here for a good few years yet, with or without The Witch's Tears.'

Hettie brightened visibly. 'Will we, Aurelia? Will we really?'

Aurelia nodded. 'We will. But it can't hurt to get a little help from Jennet now, can it? And I'd be happy to help too, if you need it.'

'I'd be very grateful, if you don't mind.'

Aurelia looked at Mia. 'Show them, Mia. Show Hettie and our friends, The Witch's Tears.'

Mia pointed towards the hedge but the kingfisher had gone.

'Er. That's a hedge,' Ella said.

'Don't ever take things at face value,' Aurelia said. 'You need to look behind to see what's really there.'

From nowhere the gentle breeze that had been wafting through the trees and hedgerows, turned into a gale force wind. The hedges around the pond bent double and branches snapped and flew through the air. Leaves spiralled like several tornadoes and within a matter of seconds what was once an overgrown hedge now revealed a rock formation overhanging a crystal-clear stream that wound its way through the copse and fed into the pond. One of the large rocks had a crack running through it and as Mia stared at it she could see quite clearly why it was called The Witch's Tears. The rock was shaped like a face. A woman's face and water from the crack seemed to be coming from the exact spot where her eyes would be.

'This is just our crazy weather, right?' Ella whispered to Mia. 'This wasn't magic or witchcraft or anything, was it?'

'Who knows?' said Mia. 'But I'm sort of hoping it's magic because there's something I want and perhaps The Witch's Tears could help me get it.'

# Chapter Twenty-Six

'I don't know if it was some sort of magic,' Mia said to Lori the following day while trying to explain about the transformation of Aurelia's garden hedge, 'or simply a weird coincidence, but it made me a believer, then and there.'

'We've been having such strange weather lately, sweetheart. All that rain in June, followed by a couple of pretty spectacular storms, then sudden showers, sunshine and more storms. Now this month we've had a heatwave. Perhaps it was the weather, or perhaps it wasn't. I suppose the only way you'll know is if you get your wish. What exactly did you wish for, or aren't you allowed to say?'

'You don't make a wish. It's not like The Wishing Tree. You have to think of what it is you want most. More than anything else in the world, and you have to imagine yourself having it, while you drink from The Witch's Tears. That's why Aurelia was so insistent that we got it right. If we let our minds wander from what it was we wanted, the chances of us getting it are zilch. Or we might end up with something we really don't want. I know you think I'm being silly because it's early days and that I'm bound to fall pregnant at some stage. But I really want a baby, Mum. More than anything in the world. And I was worrying it wouldn't happen. So that's what I asked for. A baby. I saw myself singing a lullaby to a child in my arms as I sat in one of the guest rooms upstairs. And I saw myself surrounded by happy children with Jet playing peek-a-boo and the sun pouring through the windows.'

'In other words, you asked for a happy family. Not just one baby but a few.'

Mia smiled. 'I know. I suppose it was greedy of me, but when I told Aurelia, she said it was fine. What I asked for brought happiness and joy and I asked it with a good heart, which is what The Witch's Tears is all about.'

'What did Hettie ask for? Did she ever say?'

'Eventually, yes. And that was a huge surprise. Both Ella and I had thought she might be dying or something. I couldn't believe it when I heard. Hettie's been having terrible pains in her hips and the doctor said she'd need a hip replacement. She's been worrying herself sick but she's been putting on a brave face for all of us because she didn't want to spoil my wedding, or worry anyone else. Can you believe that Hettie could keep something like that to herself? She told

Fred, of course, and swore him to secrecy. Apparently she's terrified of hospitals and she'd convinced herself that if she went in, she wouldn't come out. She simply wanted to ask to get through it. And that's when it all got even more strange.'

'Is that possible?' Lori laughed as she poured herself more coffee from the pot on the kitchen table.

'Believe me, it is. The reason Hettie and Aurelia haven't spoken for over forty years is because Hettie was desperate to have a baby. We know that's true because she told us about Hector and Elizabeth, remember.'

'Yes. And about Leo.'

'Yes. Well, Aurelia had given Hettie a bay leaf and told her to write her wish on the leaf and then burn it in the flame of a candle. Hettie did it but nothing happened. Then a year or so later, instead of her giving Hector a child, Elizabeth did, and Aurelia told Hettie it was because Hettie must've made a mistake when she did the spell. But Hettie blamed Aurelia and said that she wasn't a 'real' witch. It seems Aurelia wasn't sure she wanted to be and that's why she'd trained to be a nurse. Then her mum had died and Aurelia came back and, well, sort of took over as the resident witch.'

'Oh good heavens. You couldn't make this stuff up.'

Mia giggled but quickly became serious. 'I shouldn't laugh. It's not really funny. Hettie was heartbroken at not having a child. And I can understand that. Anyway, when they went through it again yesterday, it turns out that Aurelia didn't tell Hettie that she must let the bay leaf burn itself out. She took it for granted that Hettie would do that. And Hettie had. But Hector, seeing something burning on their kitchen table, threw a tea towel over the bowl Hettie had put the burning leaf in, and then threw the lot outside in a trough of water. Aurelia said that's why it was someone else, outside of Hettie's home, who had Hector's child. According to Aurelia, magic can not be messed around with.'

Lori burst out laughing. 'Oh dear. I'm sorry. I know I shouldn't laugh and I know it's all so terribly sad about Hettie not having children but has she truly believed all these years that the reason she couldn't was because Aurelia's spell hadn't worked?'

'She believes the curse of Frog's Hollow killed her husband, Mum. Of course she's believed that all these years. This is Hettie.'

'But why blame Aurelia? Surely if anyone was to blame for the spell going wrong it was Hector?'

'I think Hettie finally realised that yesterday. But she'd always put Hector on a pedestal. Not that he deserved it, but she had. It hadn't occurred to her that it was his fault. Anyway, Aurelia told her exactly what to ask for from The Witch's Tears and exactly what to imagine, and Hettie swears she did it right. Only time will tell but I've called a specialist this morning and arranged for Hettie to have her op done privately. She's got an appointment to meet him on Friday, and Jet and I are going with her and Fred to make sure we get all the facts.'

Lori shook her head. 'And Aurelia? Are she and Hettie friends again?'

'Only time will tell about that too, but I think they will be. Aurelia was as concerned as the rest of us, although she did call Hettie an old fool and said Hettie should've gone to see her right away.'

'Did anyone else ask The Witch's Tears for anything? Did Ella?'

'No. And not even Tabbie, which surprised me. I thought she might ask for something to happen about her and Justin, but she didn't. And Jet won't have anything to do with any of this sort of stuff. He wouldn't even have his fortune told last year, although he had told Tiffany he would. Oh. And that's another bit of news. It turns out the fortune-teller who comes here every year is only Aurelia's sister, Jezebella. Can you believe that? What a small world!'

Lori shook her head. 'To be honest, sweetheart, I'm not sure anything about Little Pondale will ever surprise me. But what happened afterwards? Did the hedge miraculously grow back and cover the rocks again?'

Mia shook her head. 'No. It seems The Witch's Tears are here to stay. At least for a while.'

'How did it get the name? You said it's called that because of Jennet de Witt.'

'It was. Although Gill said he had read something only an hour or so before we went to Aurelia's yesterday, about a place known as The Woman's Tears. We think that's why Jennet chose to build her cottage there. Because of the natural spring. Then Jennet used water from the spring to save her lover and her baby when they nearly died from some disease that swept through the village. She made them drink the water and she drank it herself and, so it says in Aurelia's family diaries passed down through the ages, because of that, they lived. But not everyone else did. And it seems Jennet's lover was married. When his wife found out, she and some of the other villagers who had lost loved ones, came to Witt's Cottage – or the Witch's Cottage as it was then called by the locals, and they dragged her and her lover out and drowned them both in the very pond that Tabbie drove her car into. At some stage after that, someone called the rock formation The Witch's Tears instead of The Woman's Tears, because of Jennet.'

'That's dreadful, sweetheart. What happened to the baby?'

'Oh. Jennet had another daughter from her previous marriage and that daughter took the baby and ran. She returned some time later when it had all calmed down but became a bit of a hermit, like Aurelia.'

'Not a complete hermit. Or was it the baby who grew up and continued the line?'

'It was the baby.'

'It's surprising then that The Witch's Tears gives people what they ask for. After the villagers dragged her and her lover out, you would think Jennet would've put a curse on the place as she was dying.'

'That's exactly what Ella said. But Aurelia says Jennet was all about the good in people. And she got what she asked for, according to the daughter who brought up her child. Jennet had often said that she wanted to die beside her lover on a warm summer's day. And she did. They died on the 26th of July 1618. So she got exactly what she asked for. Aurelia said Jennet never made mistakes with her spells, but she made a mistake with The Witch's Tears because she didn't say she wanted to die old. But it wasn't called The Witch's Tears then of course and she hadn't cast a spell, as such, according to Aurelia. It was the daughter who realised the power of the place and the magic may have been there long before Jennet arrived.'

'Hmm. I think the whole thing sounds a trifle iffy to me, sweetheart. But I truly hope you get what you want. And I hope Hettie does too. I'd like to go there to see it, but I don't think I'll be asking it for anything. Although I wouldn't be surprised if Bree does. I think she's worrying about these babies rather a lot. She's almost convincing herself something is going to go wrong.'

'Really? Then I'd better have a word with her, or get Aurelia to. Negative thoughts can be just as powerful as positive ones, Aurelia told both me and Hettie yesterday. The sooner Bree starts thinking everything will go well, the more chance there is that it will. And it will, won't it, Mum?'

'Yes sweetheart. I'm sure it will.'

'But it wouldn't do any harm if Bree got a little help from The Witch's Tears, I suppose, now would it?'

# Chapter Twenty-Seven

'Well,' said Mia, two weeks later when she and Jet were in bed. 'It seems everyone in the village has now heard about The Witch's Tears, despite each of us that day, all promising we wouldn't say a word.'

'I haven't told a soul,' Jet said, pulling her into his arms.

'And Hettie swore to Aurelia at the hospital today that no one has heard it from her.'

Jet glanced at Mia. 'Aurelia visited Hettie at the hospital?'

'Yep. Hettie was so astonished she forgot that she's in pain. Although even she says it's nowhere near as painful as she expected it to be. The op was a complete success and the doctor said that, all being well, Hettie can come home in a couple of days. I've discussed it with Fred, and also with Leo who was there as well today, and we've arranged for nurses to look after her at home.'

'I'll pop in and see her tomorrow. I hope she didn't mind that I couldn't get there today.'

'She didn't mind at all. I think she just wanted to sleep. None of us stayed long. I gave Aurelia a lift back to Witt's Cottage and there were a couple of people waiting outside when we arrived. Aurelia said that so many people were calling at the cottage lately that she was seriously considering taking a leaf out of her younger sister's book and might start charging them for the water. But I don't think she ever would. Ella told her the other day that she should bottle it, call it The Witch's Tears, and get people to pay a fortune for it and Aurelia said she could never do that.'

'I saw Garrick today and he said that Bree's feeling so much better since Aurelia gave her some herbs. No more morning sickness. No more mood swings. And no more sleepless nights. Until the babies are born. Then they'll never get any sleep. Does he know about The Witch's Tears? I didn't mention it but did Bree tell him that she went with you the other day?'

'Yes. I think so. She said she was going to and Aurelia agreed that it was okay for Garrick to know. He won't be convinced about the magic of the place, but I noticed a change in Bree as soon as the water had been drunk. It was as if a weight had lifted from her shoulders. And Ella says she's seen a difference in Bree too. When anyone asked her how she and the baby cygnets, as they've become known, thanks to Ella, were doing, Ella said a crease of worry would appear between Bree's eyes. Since The Witch's Tears, that doesn't happen.'

'That in itself should make things easier for her then. And for Garrick too.'

Mia nodded and cuddled closer to Jet.

'Tabbie's finished her blog post about Jennet de Witt, her life, her loves and her descendants, which she's called *The Witch's Tears*. I thought Aurelia might ask her to change the title but she seems fine with it. Oh, and her interview, *Dinner with Justin Lake* is going live tomorrow.'

'I've got some news about Justin, but keep it to yourself because he hasn't told Tabbie yet. Oh wait.' Jet glanced at the clock beside the bed. 'It's almost eleven so he probably has.'

'What? What is it?' Mia leant on her elbow and looked into Jet's eyes.

'He had a call about a film offer today, which means he'll have to return to L.A. in a couple of days. But he says he can't bear the thought of leaving Tabbie, so he's asking her if she'd like to continue their relationship in L.A. and see what happens.'

'Wow! That's fantastic. But not very romantic. Is he really going to use those words? "See what happens". It sounds like he's not really bothered either way.'

'He's bothered, believe me. The last time I saw a man as bothered as he is, was when I looked in a mirror soon after I met you.'

'Aw, darling! Now that's romantic.'

She kissed him on the lips and he wrapped his arms around her.

'I think what he's actually going to say is something along the lines of would she be interested in continuing their 'Summer Kisses' in the City of Angels. Her mum uses that term, apparently. He doesn't want to put too much pressure on her because she's concerned about leaving her mum, so he's trying to keep it light-hearted. But I'm telling you, Mia, he's in love. Maybe not quite as deeply as I am with you, but he's on the way, believe me.'

'They'll still be kissing come winter.'

'And for many summers and winters to come, if I know Justin at all – and I do.'

'When is he leaving? Did he say?'

'This weekend. But he says he'll pop back far more often from now on. I wouldn't be at all surprised if he moves back here you know. I don't think it'll be long before Jenny and Glen tie the knot the way their relationship is going. She'll move into Rectory Cottage which means Baker's Cottage will be free for Justin to come back to. Until he finds somewhere more suited to a Hollywood star.' Jet laughed and ran a finger across Mia's cheek.

'Well Gill's put his house in Cambridge on the market today, so it's all happening. Ella's so keen to find something in the village that she told me she wants to go to ask for help from The

Witch's Tears tomorrow. Especially after Toby announced in the pub last night that he'd asked Christy and Dylan to move in with him and was buying Hollow's End Cottage on Frog Hill Lane which had suddenly become vacant after Christy paid a visit to The Witch's Tears.'

Jet shook his head. 'Hmm. I think that had more to do with Phyllis and Peter Worrell wanting to move to warmer climes than it did with Christy drinking water from a spring, but I suppose it does no harm to ask.'

'She's going to ask for a cottage on Lily Pond Lane for her and Gill to live, love and laugh in for the rest of their days on this earth. And, because she's headed Aurelia's warning to be precise, she's going to imagine herself and Gill, two kids, one boy, one girl, a dog and a cat all sitting in the sitting room of the cottage between Sunbeam and Duckdown. Garrick said it's called Tumblewell Cottage. He says he can still remember it from the first day we all arrived here, but the sign he said he saw that day is no longer there.'

'It is called Tumblewell. I can remember that. Two kids, eh? So how many did you ask for?'

'Me?'

Jet grinned at her. 'Yes, my darling wife. That was what you asked for, wasn't it?'

Mia grinned back. 'Maybe.'

'How many?' He looked her in the eye and his grin turned into a sexy smile. 'I'm only asking because if it's more than two, we'd better make a start. These things take time and practice.'

'It was more than two,' she said. 'So stop talking, darling husband and kiss me right now.'

# Chapter Twenty-Eight

'Have you set a date for your wedding?' Mia asked Ella on the day of the annual Summer Fête.

'No. Bree's got enough on her plate what with her clients' weddings as well as planning her own and I'm running around like a mad thing trying to help her out. I'd rather concentrate on getting our cottage, but I'm leaning towards a winter wedding. I know that sounds mad but I want lots of sparkle and lights and snow, and to arrive at the church in a sleigh, drawn by your reindeer, of course. So we're thinking about December.'

'I don't think that's mad, but I do think you should get it booked in with Glen. I don't think it'll be too long before Jenny and Glen and Cathy and Leo are setting wedding dates too, so you don't want to find you can't get the date you want.'

'And Christy and Toby and Alexia and Bear. It's hard to believe that so many people have found love on Lily Pond Lane.'

'Tabbie and Justin technically found love in Aurelia's pond. He told Jet that he knew the minute he saw Tabbie after getting her car out of the pond that she was someone special. That maybe, she was 'The One'. I'm so glad she went to L.A. with him. And with her mum's blessing. Although they'll both be back for her mum's big birthday in September. And for Bree and Garrick's wedding in October.'

'Hmm. I believe they actually found love after she slapped his face in your sitting room. Or maybe I'm being too precise. I'm so careful with the little details after hearing about Hettie and Aurelia and that bloody bay leaf.'

Mia laughed. 'I know. I feel the same way.'

'Do you really believe that we'll all get what we want from The Witch's Tears? There's no time frame involved, is there? Not like The Wishing Tree.'

'I do believe it. I think. But that's why we're here. There's a certain fortune-teller I want to see and there's something I want to ask her.'

# Chapter Twenty-Nine

Mia hesitated as she approached the fortune-teller's tent. What if Jezebella told her something she didn't want to hear? But wasn't it better to know than not know? She straightened her spine, pushed her shoulders back, took a calming breath and stepped inside.

'Take a seat,' Jezebella said.

She looked at Mia as if she recognised her. But that was ridiculous. She must see thousands of people in villages all over the country. She would hardly remember Mia. Mia wondered if she should tell Jezebella that she knew who she was. But now was probably not the best time.

Jezebella stared into her crystal ball.

'I see wonderful things ahead.' She glanced across at Mia and gave her a fleeting smile. 'Fortune has indeed smiled on you, hasn't it? And now you're wondering if your luck has run out.'

How could she possibly know that? Mia shifted in her seat. But wasn't that why she was here? Because she hoped Jezebella knew everything. Because she believed Jezebella could give her the answer to the one question that was still plaguing her, in spite of The Witch's Tears.

'Yes.' Mia met Jezebella's eyes. 'I came here last year and everything you told me came true. But you said I'd have happiness and joy beyond my wildest dreams.' Mia fiddled with the black pearl bracelet Jet had bought her on their honeymoon. It had two intertwined, platinum hearts.

'Haven't you?'

'Well yes. Yes, I have.'

'But there's something else you still want?'

Mia glanced down to her lap and crossed her fingers. A ludicrous thing to do given her situation but she couldn't help herself. Suddenly, too emotional to speak, she simply nodded. When Jezebella hadn't responded after several seconds, Mia looked up and saw that she had leant back into her chair and was studying Mia intently.

'It's bad news, isn't it?'

A sardonic grin crept across Jezebella's mouth. 'What makes you say that?'

Mia fidgeted in her seat once more and her tone was raised more than she had intended when she replied: 'Because if it wasn't, you would've told me by now. And you probably would've told me last year, so the fact that you didn't must mean it's not going to happen, in spite of everything.'

'Maybe it does. Maybe it doesn't. We don't

always get everything we want, and you've got more than most.'

'I'm well aware of that. So that's it? That's all you've got to tell me?'

Jezebella shrugged and sat upright. 'I didn't say that. Patience is a virtue. And it's something you should consider. Why are you in such a rush?'

'I'm not. Not really. It's just that … Well, as I said, if it was going to happen, you probably would've told me so last year.'

Again the grin. 'No, I wouldn't. If I told you everything your future held in one sitting, you wouldn't have come back this year, would you?'

Mia's eyes and mouth grew wide. 'You mean you held something back on purpose?'

Another shrug. 'We've all got to make a living. Besides, it's not wise to tell people too much at once. They might miss something important. Like a warning, perhaps.'

She was definitely Aurelia's sister.

'So there's more? You do have something to tell me?'

Jezebella stared into her crystal ball which seemed to have grown cloudy and undergone a slight change in colour since Mia had entered the tent.

'Yes.'

'What is it?'

She shot a disapproving look at Mia from beneath her lashes. 'Patience.'

'Sorry.'

'I still see happiness and joy beyond your wildest dreams. I see a house. A large old house with several bedrooms, only one of which remains for guests. The rest are filled with laughter. It's a happy house now. A fortunate house. One that won't see sadness as other houses might.' She was silent for a second or two before leaning back in her seat once more, a crooked smile on her mouth but a twinkle in her eye that indicated she was genuinely happy. 'You'll get what you've been wishing for. You'll get it in abundance. Fortune definitely smiles on you.' She shot forward and reached across the table towards Mia, tapping the table top just in front of Mia as if trying to make her pay special attention. 'And it's not just fortune who smiles on you. Remember that. Remember her.'

'Mattie? You mean Mattie?'

Jezebella merely held her gaze without response.

'And are you saying I'll have five children? Five? It's a seven-bedroomed house, so with one for me and Jet and one for guests, that leaves five.'

Jezebella shrugged. 'I say what I see.'

'Oh my God! I'm so happy. Thank you. Thank you so much. You have no idea how much this means to me.'

'I think I do. That'll be £20 please.'

'£20? It was £15 last year. Sorry. I'm not complaining. I don't even know why I said that.' Mia grabbed her purse.

'Everything goes up. Blame Brexit, ducky. I do.'

Mia smiled and put a £50 note on the table. 'I'm so happy I think I'm actually going to cry.'

'I can't change a £50 note.'

'I don't want change. It was worth every penny.' Mia stood up and her smile grew wider.

Jezebella smiled back and it was genuine. 'That's why fortune smiles on you. Share what you have and fortune will give you more. Good luck, Mia. I wish you well. Not that you need my well-wishes.'

'You know my name!' In a way, Mia wasn't surprised.

Jezebella nodded and gave a knowing smile. 'I know everything.'

Mia grinned from ear to ear as she headed towards the August sunshine, but she stopped at the opening and turned back towards Jezebella.

'Then I don't suppose you could tell me when I might expect some news, could you?'

Jezebella raised her brows. 'I assume you're asking if I will, not if I can.'

'Absolutely. Will you tell me? Or at least give me some indication. Please.'

'You obviously didn't hear what I said about having patience.' She sounded cross, but her smile belied her tone and when she concentrated on her crystal ball she was still smiling. 'As you said "Please", I'll tell you what I see. Children are like buses. We wait and wait and suddenly they all come along, one after another. And if that isn't the answer you want, I'll also tell you this. Not this Christmas, but the next one, you'll be sharing exciting news with your husband.'

'So I'll be pregnant by not this Christmas, but the next? Thank you. Thank you. Thank you. That's fantastic news. I can't wait to tell Jet.'

'And before you ask – No. That bit won't cost you extra. That bit is free.'

Which was exactly what Jezebella had said to Mia this time last year.

'Thank you.'

'I'm surprised you needed to come here today. I thought you'd already asked for what you want. I'm glad you did. It's not often someone gives me a crisp one of these.' Jezebella smiled as she waved the money in the air. 'Oh, and if you see my sister before I do, please tell her I'm here as always, and I'll be round for supper, as usual.'

Mia's mouth dropped open in astonishment but she shook her head and smiled.

'I'll be sure to do that, Jezebella. But I think she already knows.'

Mia left the tent and beamed at Ella.

'It's your turn, Ella,' she said. 'I'll see you in half an hour at The Frog and Lily. There's something I need to tell Jet.'

'Wait! Aren't you going to tell me?'

'As much as I love you, you'll soon find out that there are some things you want to tell your husband before you tell your best friend. But I'll give you a hint. Christmases are going to be five times more expensive in the not too distant future.'

She beamed again and gave Ella a massive hug as she let her words sink in.

'Wait. What? Five times!' Ella shrieked, as Mia turned away to find Jet and break the news. 'Bloody Nora.'

# Coming soon

Well, this book was definitely the final book in my Lily Pond Lane series and I really hope you've enjoyed each one. I'll be sad to say goodbye to Mia and the gang but it's time they were left to their own devices.

There's an interactive map of Little Pondale on my website. If you haven't seen it yet, do pop over and take a look.

Thank you for all the love and support you've shown for this series. It means so much to me.

It's now time for me to continue with the other projects I'd put on hold. That means a new series which I'll tell you about very soon.

There'll be news on my website, in my newsletter, in my Facebook Readers' Club, and also via social media. Please make sure we're connected via at least one of those, to ensure you're in the know.

I'll also have a new, Christmas book out later this year and I'm working on a book I've wanted to write for a long time. I'm excited, but it's early days on that one.

# A Note from Emily

Thank you for reading this book. A little piece of my heart goes into all of my books and when I send them on their way, I really hope they bring a smile to someone's face. If this book made you smile, or gave you a few pleasant hours of relaxation, I'd love it if you would tell your friends.

I'd be really happy if you have a minute or two to post a review. Just a line will do, and a kind review makes such a difference to my day – to any author's day. Huge thanks to those of you who do so, and for your lovely comments and support on social media. Thank you.

A writer's life can be lonely at times. Sharing a virtual cup of coffee or a glass of wine, or exchanging a few friendly words on Facebook, Twitter or Instagram is so much fun.

You might like to join my Readers' Club by signing up for my newsletter. It's absolutely free, your email address is safe and won't be shared and I won't bombard you, I promise. You can enter competitions and enjoy some giveaways. In addition to that, there's my author page on Facebook and there's also a new Facebook group. You can chat with me and with other fans and get access to my book news, snippets from my daily life, early extracts from my books and lots more besides. Details are on the 'For You' page of my website. You'll find all my contact links in the

Contact section following this.
I'm working on my next book right now. Let's see where my characters take us this time. Hope to chat with you soon.

To see details of my other books, please go to the books page on my website, or scan the QR code below to see all my books on Amazon.

# Contact

If you want to be the first to hear Emily's news, find out about book releases, enter competitions and gain automatic entry into her Readers' Club, go to: https://www.emilyharvale.com and subscribe to her newsletter via the 'Sign me up' box. If you love Emily's books and want to chat with her and other fans, ask to join the exclusive Emily Harvale's Readers' Club Facebook group.

Or come and say 'Hello' on Facebook, Twitter and Instagram.

Contact Emily via social media:
www.twitter.com/emilyharvale
www.facebook.com/emilyharvalewriter
www.facebook.com/emilyharvale
www.instagram.com/emilyharvale

Or by email via the website:
www.emilyharvale.com

Printed in Great Britain
by Amazon